**LIGHTNIN' BUG
PUBLISHING**

MW00712092

The Gator and the Holy Ghost

and other Stories of a *Slightly* Reconstructed South

by James L. Fortuna, Jr.

a *Lightnin' Bug* book
Statesville, North Carolina

This is a work of fiction. All characters and events portrayed in these stories are either fictional or used fictitiously. Any similarities to persons living or dead are coincidental and probably not intended as satire.

The Gator and the Holy Ghost and Other Stories from a Slightly Reconstructed South

Copyright © 2012 by James L. Fortuna, Jr.

All rights reserved. No part of this book may be used or reproduced without written permission from the author except in the case of brief quotations included in articles and reviews.

First Electronic Publication, Lightnin' Bug Publishing, 2012

First Trade Publication, Lightnin' Bug Publishing, 2014

ISBN-13: 978-0-9881929-2-8

A Lightnin' Bug book

Lightnin' Bug Publishing
Statesville, NC 28625
Lightninbug@att.net

Cover Illustration: "Gator can't drive" Copyright © 2012 by Carolyn A. Fortuna. Used with permission.

Lyrics to "Hound Dog" quoted in "An Ancient Enemy" are by Jerry Leiber and Mike Stoller

This book is dedicated to Kathleen S. Fortuna

TABLE OF CONTENTS

PREFACE

The dubiously named social re-engineering policies known collectively as Reconstruction turned Southern culture on its head; proud people accustomed to liberty and autonomy found themselves occupied and manipulated by what was, by any meaningful standard, a foreign power. The impotence created by Reconstruction policies is the root of the angst that pervades the Southern spirit into the Twenty-First Century and that resonates in the stories and vignettes in James L. Fortuna Jr.'s collection, *The Gator and the Holy Ghost and Other Stories from a Slightly Reconstructed South.*

The War Between the States was simply about slavery, we're told; the virtuous Union Army prevailed against evil slavers to bring freedom and justice to all men, or so we were taught in every American History course since 1870. Fortuna's stories remind us that nothing is simple, that no political action or social philosophy exists in a vacuum, that everything has its contexts. He illustrates the shame and despair underpinning the Southern soul compassionately, humorously, and—always-- honestly.

Fortuna's work draws on a lifetime in the South spent listening to its people and feeling the social upheaval that has shaped and disoriented his generation. He writes in the voices of the characters in his life and illuminates the archetypal humanity in fear, folly, and faith.

Fortuna's is a genuine Southern voice that readers will find both unique and affective, evoking sensibilities reminiscent of Faulkner and O'Connor and grotesqueries reminiscent of Kafka. The stories in this collection are lyrical, dense with meaning and emotion, and rich with unforgettable characters who embody the best and worst of the post-reconstruction South.

Christopher Brincefield, May, 2012

Prince of the Power of the Air

Lazer Mullins saw The Devil on a TV show a week ago. He saw him plain and clear and in color on the back row of the Jack Onan Ministries, Inc.'s Full Revival Chorus, singing along with what seemed to be true joy and fervor on that most famous of sacred songs, *I'll Fly Away.* Lazer was sure of who it was, too. No mistake at all. The Devil.

"I seen him, OK," he said in a whisper to his girlfriend, Lola Preston, between bites of a medium rare Whiz-O-Burger with extra cheese and onions. They sat facing each other in the back booth at the Rainbow Good Eats on a slow Saturday evening, late August, in Slackbridge, Georgia. "I knowed it was him first time they showed his face." Lazer ate some more, chewing quickly and swallowing almost in the same motion, thinking along with it all of the Devil on the back row.

"How can you be so sure?" Lola sipped at a cherry cola and tried to figure out where all this was heading. She and Lazer had gone together for almost two years now, and she knew too well how he seemed to start out small and go so big that nobody else could follow. She'd seen it many times. She didn't like this Devil thing at all.

"Oh it was him, OK. I knowed that right off. It flashed on me when his face come clear that first time." Lazer munched at an undersized French-fry and frowned. "He was full of blood."

"Do what?" Lola glanced at her watch and decided to cut the evening short. Lazer was rolling hard. Straight ahead toward a place he probably wasn't even sure was there at all. The jukebox across the room tried to sing—lit up for a moment, clanked and groaned and died. Somebody new had tried it out. A real sucker. Lazer didn't seem to notice.

"Blood—like a tick. Full up with it. And smiling too—big front teeth pointed right at the people's faces. I seen it all." Lazer popped three fries into his mouth and suck-chewed them out of sight. "They can't fool me."

"They?" Up front, a blond-haired man in a red cowboy shirt was trying to pay the cashier. He kept dropping his change. The Good Eats was getting ready to close. And tomorrow was Sunday, Lola's day to sleep in past dawn. "What do you mean, 'they'?"

"Them preachers over there at the Temple. That Onan and them others. They can't fool me none. I know what they're up to. Pretty damn slick too." He laughed and shook his head and grabbed at the burger with both hands.

"Fool you? Lazer, why'd they..." Lola looked close at Lazer's eyes and shut up. He was near gone as it was and more words might just make it never stop. She was tired anyway. Her feet hurt. But Lazer didn't care about that. Not a bit. Not while he was rolling on toward wherever it was he was heading. They both worked for Silver Needles. Sewing jobs. Production. But only she seemed to notice or be bothered by how miserable it was. Or how she wanted to get married again and make a home for somebody. For Lazer. But he just wouldn't quit rolling on long enough for any of that. The cowboy up front finally paid his bill. Lazer and Lola were the only customer's left.

"I'm sure of what I saw. I ain't kidding here." Lazer slurped down about half of a strawberry shake and waved away the short-legged waitress who had clomped back to see how close to done they were. "Yes sir I ain't kidding one little bit."

"I know." Lola sighed and reached for her purse. "You about ready?" But his eyes were nowhere near it. She could see that little flicker along the bottom rim growing stronger as he took care of the burger and went after the last dregs of his shake. The few remaining fries were massed on the side of his plate, perhaps free from further harm.

"Oh I'm ready, OK. Ready. They can't do that, y'know."

"I need to get on home now, Lazer." Lola put down two crushed one dollar bills near the ketchup bottle and motioned to the stumpy waitress. "I'll go pay. OK?"

"They can't just let the Devil come on TV like that. It ain't legal. Something. It ain't suppose to be. Right?" He was staring at the table, at the spilled salt near the napkin holder. At the wide and glistening ketchup pool near the edge of his plate. At whatever it was he stared at when he got rolling good and strong.

"I'll go pay, Lazer. An' get a cab or something. Call me tomorrow. I'm going to church at Mt. Pisgah. OK? Call me." She slid out and free. Again. Nearly two years of sweetness mostly but bruised and broken into by the rolling-on and pure old craziness that was getting worse and worse. She now just felt mostly sorry for him. No family. Parents dead. One brother killed in Viet Nam and the other one by a deputy over in Ailey. Living in the boarding house with them old people. Lola sighed and brushed at her hair. Her Mama was right, she decided, as she paid the bill and turned to leave. The cowboy was outside, smoking a cigar and smiling at her through the greasy-looking glass of the big front door. Her Mama was right. Past time to move on.

***

It was hot outside. Lazer moved through the deep hot-and-sticky like he was swimming in a dream. Lola was gone. He couldn't remember her leaving. The waitress had said the bill was already paid. And he was finally nudged toward the door by the grill cook, Big Bo:

"Past closing there, Lazer. Late, buddy. Get on home now."

"Yeah yeah. Home." But Lazer didn't go there. To his room at the end of a long hall and into the night sounds. The snores and groans and whimpers all around him and worse the closer on to dawn it came. He drove instead to the main gate of the Onan Ministries, Inc.'s Full American Home of the Holy Ghost, parked on a small rise of pine and scrub-wooded land across the highway out of sight of the first guard tower, and watched the multi-colored spotlights flicker across the pines and up along the big chain-link fence out front.

"He's in there by God." He muttered and drummed his fingertips on the dented steering wheel. It was hotter now even than when he left the Good Eats. He rubbed his eyes and blinked a few times against sleep trying hard to settle in. It was lonely, felt lonely there, and he wondered where Lola had gone. With him one minute and gone the next. Never coming back. Like always. Like everybody. Not the Devil though. Not him. He never stayed away. Lazer had seen him four times before now. At a distance. Always too far away to get to. Just stirring things up mostly. Causing trouble. Making things harder on Lazer. Making him sin. Sucking him in. Lola'd never understand none of that. She was never no real help anyways. Her and that scrawny, no-toothed mama of hers. No help in much of anything and for damn sure no help in this business he was thinking about getting into right here. The colored lights seemed to float across the treetops and then bob and bounce like tied-up balloons out behind a slow-moving wagon. It looked crazy over there. Just like Preacher Onan and his fat wife. And the Devil he let in to sing. Lazer rubbed his eyes some more and fell asleep.

***

The sun was already too hot but only just a little ways above the trees. A dry-fly woke Lazer up. He must have rolled on it or somehow punched it in his sleep. The scream brought him straight up from the seat. His mouth felt like something had peeled off a layer of skin and lightly dusted what was left with salt. A rusty taste was there too but further down his throat. Sunday morning.

"Sweet Jesus lookit all that." He whistled lowly after the last word got out and then sat awhile staring down toward the highway, watching the seemingly endless line of cars coming slowly from both directions and meeting at the front gate to form a single line into the Home of the Holy Ghost. The gate was open and guards in sports coats were busy checking the people through. A huge banner stretching over the gold-painted inner road spelled out: HEAVEN'S OWN. "He's in there, by God—I can feel it."

Lazer started the engine on the second try, eased out of the scrub and brush, and rolled down to the main highway. He had to wait a few minutes before a Christian let him into line just two cars from the guards. His mouth still felt rough, taste all screwed up and that rust-flavor mostly taking charge. The guards looked like they knew nothing about who was singing inside. Like it was nothing at all that the damn Devil himself was part of all the smoke and lights that Preacher Onan put out. Lazer smiled real big at the first guard, a fat black boy whose face looked too small for the rest of him.

"You a regular or new-found? I don't see no de-cal." The guard's voice was loud and steady, like one of them machine voices on the phone.

"What?" Lazer didn't like the fat boy. He looked a little like Lola's ex-husband, a drunk who sometimes swept up at the plant. He had tried to fight Lazer one night over some damn thing or other. Lazer busted a broom handle over his head and kicked him once or twice. That was pretty much it. Lola had been grateful though. That's how they met. He'd forgotten that. The fat boy was trying to smile.

"You new—first-time visitor? Or a regular member?"

"I ain't never been here before if that's what…"

"OK—here, "he handed Lazer a bright orange smiling sun with a red cross drawn down its middle. "Put this on the inside of your window here in front and drive on through. You get special parking as a new-found—signs'll show you. Praise Jesus!"

"Yeah yeah." Praise Lucifer was more like it, Lazer thought. What with the man himself all big and smiley up yonder on the back row of that chorus. All full of blood and looking to get more. On TV big as life. Lazer thought about all that as he followed a mini-van with a THERE'S NO GOD LIKE MY GOD sticker across its dented back. Slowing, he reached in the glove compartment, pulled out a snub-nosed .38 and pushed it under his shirt, down inside his belt, cool metal resting against his belly. "That'll do it," he said and thought ahead to how surprised Satan would be to see a pistol coming at him from the peanut gallery.

Lazer braked as the mini-van turned right. Up ahead, the signs were confusing and he finally settled for one with a picture of some kind of cave on it and rolled up to a ramp nobody seemed to be using. Getting out, the door swung back and bumped his thigh pretty hard, and as he limped up the ramp, a gold-suited man with slicked back red hair got him into a wheelchair and started rolling him toward some tall white doors with purple doves painted on them. "Hey look," Lazer tried to turn around, "Hey—I don't need no damn…" But the man pushed him on through the doors and onto the main floor of the Onan Love Temple, into a red-carpeted, brass-rail enclosed open space to the right of the cameras, not far from the golden pulpit and over near a ramp that seemed much steeper than the one outside. The space was full of cripples and sideshow freaks. Mostly they were sitting around and drooling and cooing and bobbing their heads like a covey of insane quail gone too far into the brush. Some were thrashing out with their arms and legs, and a few were barking and oozing pus and crawling on the floor. Nurses were with them, down among the mob, starched caps on their heads and wearing blue capes. Good-looking women too, he noticed, as he tried to get up out of his chair.

"Whoa, brother—whoa now. Not time for that yet. Healing's on the way, though." The red-haired man pushed down hard on Lazer's shoulders and turned him over to a long-haired, big-busted woman who smelled like roasting coffee. "This here's brother— brother—I'm sorry, brother, but I never did get your name."

Lazer just sat there and watched an enormous headed boy/girl try to sit up while its nurse shouted encouragement. Outside the brass rails, the Temple was filling up, all three levels, and in the rows close by, the people were staring open-mouthed at the rolling, cackling freak show. Lazer patted at the gun handle beneath his shirt and tried again to get up.

"No, brother—not yet. Wait on the Holy Ghost." The nurse's voice was low, husky-sounding, and she came in close to Lazer's face, her full lips painted some shade of deep red he wasn't sure he had ever seen before. She smelled now like peanut butter as she pressed his shoulders with her long fingers and smiled. Her teeth were big. "You'll get your healing sure—anxious as you are—you'll make it quick to the hem of His garment—I just know you will. Right, Brother Kenny?"

"Amen, Sister Gabriella. Amen. Now—what's your name, Brother?" He stepped back and cocked his head like a dog puzzling out a strange noise. "Brother?"

"I—I'm Lazer. Lazer Mullins—I—" He wanted to say more, wanted to warn somebody about you-know-who, but right then the lights went low and trumpets and drums brought in Preacher Onan—his fat wife and him coming down from the top row of seats and dancing behind about forty or fifty preacher-boys dressed all in powder-blue suits that sparkled and flashed when they moved.

"Praise God praise God praise God!" Lazer's nurse was screaming and jumping up and down, "Praise God oh praise oh praise His Holy Name praise praise God!" And then she bent over and shouted in Lazer's ear, "How bad do you want your healing, honey? How bad do you want to get well?"

***

It was all going too fast, he finally decided. Too fast. Too much going on. Clog- dancers. Jugglers. Stilt-walking angels. Just like on TV whenever Lazer made a mistake and came down on the Onan Channel. A bunch of black kids in African-looking robes suddenly began to sing something nobody but them could understand. Lazer tried to keep clear of a pus-oozer, a dirty-haired *it* that kept trying to climb up on his lap. The nurse had gone to get a preacher-boy to take down Lazer's testimony.

"Here he is, Preacher Willy. This is Brother Lazer." The nurse's teeth showed bigger than before.

"Praise God, Brother Lazarus—praise God!" The boy's face was thin and pock-marked, a few scars across his cheeks making him look like he had been tattooed.

"I'm Lazer—not no Lazarus." Lazer heard the chorus begin singing somewhere past the glare and lights straight ahead, up the ramp and on past the golden pulpit up high.

"How old are you, Brother Lazarus? How old?" And the questions kept coming. Right in his ear. The preacher-boy's lips real close. He smelled like toothpaste. "Are you saved, Brother? Are you saved?" A few of the prettiest freaks were in the same spot, other nurses and their preacher-boys flapping around them like feeding buzzards, but most were being herded back behind a curtain and out of sight. The questions kept coming. The nurse was now mixing in pretty good and smelling like French-fries as she came. "Tell us, honey—we need to know—tell us now." The chorus was getting stronger by the second. Satan's own. Lazer stood up.

"Brother Lazarus—Brother—we need you to sign this form here—" The preacher-boy sounded whiny, like a mosquito out behind as Lazer started up the ramp. But the nurse's voice was the last one he heard. The gun felt good in his hand. "Honey it ain't time. It ain't time—"

***

At first, it was just bright up on the big stage, lights blazing down on him and up at him and Preacher Onan's face (and his fat wife's too) going in and out of focus as the two of them turned and saw the gun and began to dance back and forth at the pulpit like the floor was on fire. And then it just got hot—the heat like furnace flames fanning out around him as he stumbled over a rough spot on the floor behind the pulpit and came back straight right at the Devil's own place. Behind Lazer, it was dead feeling, the crowd gone all quiet now and only a few crying babies there in among the calm. Lazer never turned around but pointed the gun at the chorus and watched the people jump. Big ones and little ones, black and white and red and yellow, all bouncing side to side or dropping down and out of sight as best they could. The gun felt hot in Lazer's hand and sweat was pouring down his face. The Devil didn't move.

"Whoa there—I see you you sum-bitch—I see you!" Lazer's voice rattled out over a dangling microphone near the director's empty stand. It was still quiet in the Temple and guards were creeping up the ramps on either side of the stage. Lazer waved the gun at them and they stopped. Preacher Onan and the Mrs. had disappeared. "You grinning piece of shit—I got you!" Lazer shifted the gun to his left hand and wiped at his face.

The Devil was laughing: "You got nothing, " he said, blood-bloated cheeks jiggling and yellow teeth clacking like old dry bones rattled together in a sack or leafless tree limbs come together on a windy night. "You got nothing." The blood-face turned into a Jack-O-Lantern, light flickering inside and shadowing up the eyes. And then the Jack-O-Lantern began to float up a bit off the back row and hang in the air, hissing and spitting like a rough-used cat. "You—got—no—thing—" The words seemed to float as well and Lazer pulled the trigger five quick times and five more but nothing came of it, no fire in the gun at all. So he screamed and threw it at the floating face, and fifteen guards piled on, bringing him down hard while the people in the Temple came back alive and cheered.

The Devil walked away. Lazer saw it plain and clear as he himself was pulled up and handcuffed to the biggest guard. The Devil walked away, dressed up now in powder blue like a preacher-boy and moving slow and steady down to the nearest exit behind the stage and gone.

***

Lola saw the whole show. In the Super 8 Motel. The TV was turned down but she saw Lazer and just a little tiny flash of the Devil's face before it got away. But it all happened too quick to think about. There and gone. Like the chance to go to church. She'd make it next week for sure. She needed sleep right now. The screen went blank just as the cowboy began to snore softly beside her in the semi-dark.

Break of Day at the Woodbine, Georgia, Pecan Paradise and Cheap Gas

The office is comfortable. Ros Lytton sits facing the priest, a funny-looking curved desk between them with a small computer screen and some sort of frosted globe resting near the telephone unit. The priest is a jolly sort of man, flushed face and eyes like plump raisins pushed too far into a thick cookie dough. It is immediately clear that he likes to talk.

"Glad you're here, Mister—uh—Lytton. Glad you're here. Trouble, is it? Some sort of trouble? You said, 'trouble,' on the phone, I think. Yes? When you called?"

Ros leans back in his chair, back into the soft deep cushions and tries to remember the conversation earlier that morning. And then he tries, just for a few seconds, to bring back Woodbine, Georgia, and the true and very beginning of it all. But Woodbine won't stay and the phone dialogue from earlier that day seems like a hard try at not making sense:

"Is this Father Mitten?"

"Yes. Yes, it is."

"Father, I'm not one of your sheep—but—well I—oh no—no, I'm probably not a sheep at all. That's possible. Not a fully-grown sheep, you see—*but* there could be some sheep in me—I sometimes think so—and—well—in the meantime—I—I am at least a poor little lamb that has lost its way—daily growing, Father—*baa-baa-baa*— are you there, Father?"

"Trouble, yes? Trouble? That's it, isn't it?"

"I—I—*baa-baa-baa*—"

Ros remembers picking the church at random, St.Gadarene's Episcopal, from the yellow pages in the motel phone book. Slackbridge, Georgia, had many churches to choose from, but St. Gadarene's had a large cartoon angel in its ad that caught his eye. The angel was juggling what looked to be undersized pumpkins. Ros gives up on remembering and tunes back in on Father Mitten.

"Yes, indeed, Mr. Little. I'm glad you're here. Would you like to smoke?"

"What?"

"Smoke—you can, you know. Yes. I don't mind a bit. Go ahead, if it'll help. There's an ashtray right there. See it?"

"Here?" Ros carefully touches a ceramic-feeling red frog whose mouth is oversized and vaguely sinister.

"Yes by all means go ahead. Smoke away. I'm not one of those smoker-bashers, y'know. Not here. Not in Slackbridge. Home of Georgia Gal Cigars. Nosir. Tobacco's our good good friend hereabouts." And he smiles broadly and bites sharply a few times on his lower lip. "Now I don't smoke myself, you understand. Never have. But you go right ahead, Mr. Ludden. You just go right ahead."

"I—I don't smoke." Ros begins to regret calling the jolly priest and tries to find a nice and easy way to retreat to the Ace High Motel in time for an early dinner and maybe a drink or two of scotch before he tries to sleep. He is already a day late, and the road up ahead is full of bad memories. So he is seriously trying to begin to leave the office when he hears himself undercut that decision in the strongest way possible: "I don't think much of Camden County, and I (of course) now blame Woodbine for maybe starting up all the other sins of my past life and especially those I can't seem to get a handle on in a satisfactory way. That's why I'm here. That's why I'm here and mostly staying put. It was the Pecan Paradise and Cheap Gas, Father. That's where it began."

"The trouble?" The priest carefully frowns, eyebrows nearly touching above his red nose.

"Yes. Yes, it began there. At the gas pumps. In summer time. Dawn. Or close to it. Late June. Maybe June 28th. That seems like a nice number. It fits ok. It fits." And it does. It fits. Feels of a piece with the other almost-memories Ros always tries to bring together to explain why he can't stay free of trouble. "June 28th. 19—I think—55. I think it was 1955 but no one else agrees. None of the family thinks that. But I do. Most think it was 1956 and one cousin claims he was there and it was 1957. But he couldn't have been there, Father, don't you see, since he wasn't even born until 1958. I checked that out, Father—last year." On a quick escape from the Olustee Rehab.

Center—before his brother finally found him trying to swim the St. Mary's River naked and singing *Michael Row the Boat Ashore*. That one was his thirty-second escape. This one here is the thirty-third. He steals money to finance every one. From visitors and from the canteen. It's easy. He's a good thief. Cars especially—big blue ones are his favorites. His brother has lots of cars.

"So—Woodbine, is it? Right? Woodbine. Woodbine. Up the road here. Yes? About sixty miles north. Woodbine."

"Yes, Father."

"I've been there," the jolly priest licks his lips and half-smiles, "I know Woodbine. No. No trouble there, my boy. Is it a potato maybe? Is it made of gum? Would you like to dance?"

"What?" Ros feels his ears begin to burn. The priest is not making sense. The priest is fading rapidly into a bumpy ride along the years most recent, twenty odd spread evenly down among the good doctors and nice nurses and the big-fat-men-in-white who sometimes punch Ros in the face. The pictures thrown up are framed in steel, in blue-steel-looking lines, and move in living color, jerkily floating before a rolling backdrop of bloated clouds. Father Mitten keeps on talking. But the pictures are all Ros sees.

> PICTURE #1: The first good doctor, fat and jolly (like Father Mitten only more so), telling Ros that all things will come right again, will make a sense that he can live within without a constant charge for daily use. The first good doctor smiles and smiles full fat face at the camera or audience or whatever is there in

front but never really seen. He gives Ros drugs and lets him watch the nice nurses change their clothes.

PICTURE #2: Ros's brother, Daniel "Po'Boy" Lytton III, selling a big ol' car to some froggy-looking man in short pants and a t-shirt that says—*I got mine at Jax Beach*. Po'Boy is smiling big and his face is turned three-quarters to the front and the froggy-man looks real grateful. Po'Boy pays all Ros's bills and sometimes slips him a little whiskey when the nice nurses and big-fat-men-in white don't care.

PICTURE #3: The Olustee Rehab. Center with a round thing up over the third smokestack from the end, a thing like somebody's straw hat that maybe got sat on and then tugged and prodded back into another shape. The Center is faded brick and ivy-splayed along its front like an apron gone crazy, and the round thing seems to disappear if you close one eye. Ros has lived there (not counting escape and court time) for over twenty years.

PICTURE #4: The family. Pa. Ma. Po'Boy. Ros. Buster the three-legged dog and P.P. the cat with a torn ear and one paw bigger than the other three. It looks like old times and maybe just beyond. Maybe right after Woodbine with the trouble come from there, hiding slick somewhere inside or right around Ros close enough to touch.

Father Mitten shakes his head. The bloated clouds fall into his words, fall into nothing:

"Is Woodbine your home, my boy? Do you come from there?"

"I'm sorry, Father—I wasn't paying strict attention. Did you say something?" A few puffs of the last cloud, a particularly fat one, refuse to stay down; the priest's face is obscured by their attempts to rise.

"I said, is Woodbine your home?"

"Good God no, Father!" The puffs go fast and don't come back. "No no—why did you think that?"

"Well I just thought that since you mentioned that particular place that perhaps it was a native land or launching pad toward the grand and sincere person you have become. Would you have a piece of coal, my boy?" The priest's face fuzzes a little. Ros tries to make it clearer but can't and gives up for a while. Leaves it alone. Waits.

This time it is sounds that come. Voices and words stretching back as far as he can guess. Back maybe (he thinks whenever he hears them) all the way to the moist and sticky rim of his own beginnings. And back and forth. The priest fades again, face fuzzy and then pleasant but worried-looking. The sound is pure. The sound is always pure.

Lit-tle lit-tle—coo coo now coo
You mind Black Annie now, y'hear?

Naw suh naw suh he ain't been bad
They're niggers, son. You mind that now!
Lit-tle lit-tle—coo coo coo---

The jolly priest seems content to chew gently on his lower lip and glance ever so slyly at his wristwatch. Ros has seen this before, this sort of behavior in the face of the overwhelming nature of the presentation of the facts. Of true facts. It *is* overwhelming. The priest smiles suddenly and Ros jumps in with a question of his own.

"How come good men have to suffer?"

Ros always saves this question for the quickly-sliding-toward-the-end part of a session. He has had many sessions in the years since Woodbine. Each one more empty than the last. Always with pastors or holy men. And sometimes their wives. *Assembly of God. Church of God. Seventh-Day Adventists. Baptist (twenty-four different kinds). A.M.E. Zion. House of David. Latter-Day Saints. Methodist. Jehovah's Witnesses. Church of Christ in Perpetual Salvation, Inc.* That last one is Ros's favorite. He lived with the pastor (a video game repairman who owned his own church) for a month before his brother tracked him down and the big-fat-men-in-white caught him in the river and took him on back home. That was the last time he got free. A year ago. He thinks hard about the other pastors. A list forms quick and hot. Like always: *Presbyterian (three kinds). Holiness (all kinds—ten, he thinks at last count—he goes over the list to be sure—yes, ten). Unitarian-Universalist. Free-Range Trinitarians.* Dreamers and schemers and banana peelers and Ros there asking that one question that never quite gets answered. But in all the lists no Episcopals. Until now (the newest escape in a big,

navy blue Pontiac from Po'Boy's southwest lot)—no Episcopals at all. So he asks again a little louder as the first reel
of a movie starts flickering in his head: Woodbine not quite
clear but the years between the Pecan Paradise and
Cheap Gas—between that and the rolling mess of big trouble that finally got Po'Boy to "take charge" and "put that nut
where he belongs"—all those years just about to flicker into
a kind of life on that screen he sometimes sees behind his
eyes.

"Why, Father? Huh? Why?"

"Pardon me, my boy—did you say something?"

"I've said many somethings, Father. Yes."

"Look here—I have a wedding rehearsal over at the
church in a half-hour. And Vespers—and—well—if you
don't have anything to ask me or discuss with me or otherwise engage my attention beyond your rather brief and
ragged introduction of yourself, a mumbled reference to
Woodpiles or Woodbins or something, and the raising and
lowering of your eyebrows and then sticking out your
tongue as you have been doing for the past fifteen
minutes—if—if you cannot do more than that, I—"

Ros shakes his head. Again. Nothing gets through
again. There you have it. Again. Eyebrows and tongues but
no true sound. Again. It ends soon. At least there's that. It
comes to an end and this time just a few miles from his
destination. His perhaps ultimate destination. Back finally to
the Pecan Paradise and Cheap Gas. Over forty years later
like a broken salmon with few clear reference points and
left to swim on lust alone. It is nearly over. The priest
phones someone, and they phone someone and on and on

until Po'Boy answers, and one more time the big-fat-men appear. The priest puts down the phone. And waits. Stares at Ros and swallows hard a few good times. A siren sounds from far away, an almost dreamy whine like a bloated mosquito on the far side of a pitch black room.

"Stop that now! You stop that sort of thing! I will not sit here and be gestured at in an obscene way—stop it!"

The priest nearly bounces in his chair. Ros half-closes his eyes and lets the film roll: Glimpses are there. Only grainy glimpses of himself and the bad bad things he used to do. The siren is closer, whining much stronger and louder than before.

> ---stealing—always stealing—candy at first and nearly every time candy cigarettes and cigars and chocolate money—shiny gold and silver-covered chocolate coins—nickels and dimes and quarters—glimpses—years of glimpses—

> Stealing—and police and detention centers and doctors smiling down at him—and preachers a few times red-faced and sweating fierce to bring him home to Jesus safe and whole---

> STEALING—older then—in the next scenes—more grown-up—real cigarettes and cigars and lots of silver change—dollars even a couple of times from a newsstand down in New Smyrna Beach—Fernandina Beach too— and one time fifty rolls of quarters from an ice cream igloo on the Old St. Augustine Road—

And then he discovered cars—blue ones mostly—
big and shiny—Po'Boy's cars—and he'd
load up (Ros, not Po'Boy—Po'Boy never did
nothing bad in his whole life, Mama always
said)—Ros'd load up on cigars and cigarettes and change and try to make it to
Camden County and Woodbine and the Pecan Paradise and Cheap Gas and the
chance maybe to redo, to reverse and make
it so the old man never gets cut down and
Daddy never just drives off north to Aunt
Kathleen's beach house for the week-long
Lytton Family Reunion. Ros stays awake
most of that week, the old man's head a pink
melon there in the darkness each and every
night. Like a flashbulb balloon of moving
bright even when Ros shuts his eyes and
tries to hide. And the pink balloon stays
there forever, he thinks, and needs cigars
and cigarettes and silver change to make it
go away.

But Ros never makes it back to Woodbine. Never quite
gets there. Po'Boy or some damn thing always stops him.
The priest is new, but it's the same old thing no matter
who's there close enough to touch. Ros reaches for the
priest. The door comes open hard over behind a great big
globe of the world. Two fat-faces-all-in-brown come puffing
in and try to make it through the rolling film.

"Father Mitten—you ok?"

"Hey you—police here! Stay where you are! Don't
move!"

"Get 'em hands up where I can see 'em, buddy-row! Hey!"

"What you on, boy? What you taken?"

The fat-faces-all-in-brown and the priest seem boiling in and out of Woodbine, the film strong now and the scene as clear as if he sits for real behind his father in the old Hudson Hornet, in the deep backseat with Po'Boy fiddling with his shirt collar over at the other window behind their mother who leans forward perhaps the better to see the giant crowned pecan sitting on a gilded throne out near an ice-house painted deep red. Or perhaps she was trying to adjust the small rebel flag they had attached to the Hornet's antenna. It's not clear, not anymore, Mama just a blur at first. It's early in the morning though, just daybreak or a little past, and steam is rising up from everywhere, hot already and fixing to get much worse before long.

Ros thinks he saw the old man first, black and shiny, a gray hat in one hand and two cigars and a pack of cigarettes in the other. He kind of drops down gently onto the rough asphalt outside the office beside the garage doors about fifteen or twenty yards away. Smilin' Jimmy is looking in the car window about the same time Ros notices the old man begin to slip and slide his feet on across the asphalt toward the gas pumps island. He looks real skinny. Flags are flapping everywhere in a sudden stir of breeze and the place is empty except for the Hudson. Daddy's in a real good mood. Tapping on the steering wheel and nodding his head. Smilin' Jimmy speaks first.

"Hidy there—filler up?"

"Yes sir. Gimme the best you got, my friend."

"Jus' call me Smilin' Jimmy—everybody does."

And Ros hears his father's laugh and tries to get a better look at the black man sliding closer and closer. He looks real old. Po'Boy notices nothing but his fly and starts in unzipping and zipping it in time to some tune he must be humming in his head.

"Smilin' Jimmy, huh? You own this here?"

"Yes sir, I do. Ever bit of it. How you like my pecan over yonder,ma'am?" Nodding toward Mama a quick twitch of his head.

"It's something."

"Yes sir—the ladies seem to like it a whole lot—yes sir." Back to Daddy then: "You folks goin' far?"

"Over to Claxton Beach."

"Claxton, huh? I been there plenty times."

The old man is nearly even with the Hudson, coming in from behind and a little to the left of the back window. Ros watches close as Smilin' Jimmy turns and notices he is there. Smilin' Jimmy's face is red. Deep red with little white whirls around the dirty blue of his faded collar. The rebel flag begins to flap out a little way across the front window on Mama's side, and Smilin' Jimmy notices that too and makes a funny salute with his left hand before he turns to face the old man for real.

"Fo' d'smokes, Cap'n." As he rattles some change in his free hand, the old man's voice is gravely and low and kind of chuckles at the end.

"You jus' he'p yo'se'f there, nigger? You jus' go in my place an' he'p yo'se'f?"

"Why yessuh—I—allus jus' goes an'—"

But he never finishes. Smilin' Jimmy glances down at us and then at the rebel flag again, a quick sweep, the fingers of his left hand resting on his front shirt pocket near some red stitching with 'Jimmy' on it in a curved and twisted scrawl. Ros can touch the old man's elbow. He's that close outside the window. And he can see Smilin' Jimmy's face and watches Daddy turn toward what's going on. Mama stares out at the highway and Po'Boy's still humming along with his zipper when it starts to happen.

Smilin' Jimmy's fingers barely fall from his shirt, a flicker of a movement from the little pocket into a fist that punches full hard into the old man's blackness, hard with a splat and a little crack and crunch and bits of jagged red and then everything goes away from the window and Ros has to crane his neck to see what happens next. Mama turns toward the backseat and tries to yell or scream but nothing comes out but a little soft sucking sound like maybe she has something stuck in her throat. Daddy turns away and begins looking mostly straight ahead, hands gripped tight on the wheel and only just once or twice glancing to the left, the whole time pretending he isn't noticing a thing out of the ordinary. Mama keeps on sucking loud and Po'Boy hasn't yet even noticed that nothing is right and won't ever be right again. Outside, the old man falls down hard onto the steaming asphalt and Smilin' Jimmy kicks and kicks and kicks him—head and belly and lower down too and back on up to the head and soon it all just gets mostly pink and like a cracked melon and the steam goes thick and a sizzling sound flies up and dies down quick and Smilin' Jimmy's back in the window beside Daddy, bending down and asking again: "Fill'er up?"

The car cranks up. He hears it plain. Outside and inside both. All full and its windows cleaned. Nothing is said about the old man except for a half-muffled "niggers" that Smilin' Jimmy pushes out as he rubs his fists along his pants legs and waits on Daddy to hand him the gas money. Mama is sobbing softly and again looked away toward the highway. Po'Boy has fallen asleep. The old man is trying to crawl, his head lopsided and cigars and cigarettes and change clearly visible out the back window. Smilin' Jimmy kicks him a few more times and he quits moving. Ros watches steady until Daddy yells at him to sit down and then guns the Hudson for all she's worth. Getting away. Far away. Rebel flag flapping and Po'Boy snoring and Mama whimpering and Ros himself like Daddy never making a sound.

The film slows down and the priest opens a door and lets in a new batch of helpers. Fat-faces-in-white who punch and kick and get Ros all snug down inside a county jacket. The priest frowns and shakes his head and watches Ros go by, face full-pressed against the window of the moving car.

Two Roads South

-1-

"Red-Man Waters"

About High Sheriff Red-Man Waters the stories were thick and many-sided and most times not connected much at all to anything like a structure or a form. Episodes. Anecdotes. Bits and pieces like colored glass on a short-grass shoulder of the road, all sparkle and little surface to hold to. Most were told by the old men who worked the polls every election—the Sheriff's own—hired watchers and vote counters and the rest. They mostly gave little glimpses into the how he came south from Georgia and also sometimes into the why: He worked on the railroad and he saw a need for law and order down along the St. John's River that only he could meet in full. So he left the Seaboard Line and settled into becoming the longest running sheriff in North Florida history: nearly thirty years.

I saw him many times while I was growing up. He'd come to our elementary school and, standing tall and straight, red face smiling beneath an outsized cowboy hat, talk about the clean life and safety in the water and how to be a citizen good and true. Later on, by the time I reached high school, he'd talk how we'd never have no "nigger mess" like what was popping up all over the South in 1958 as long as he wore the badge. Grandpa liked that kind of talk. I lived with him and Granny then, while my parents were on the road with the old Sullivan Brothers Carnival. They ran a duck-bobbing game and told weights and birthdays. Grandpa hated all that as well, but hated worse what was happening to the South and so always voted for the High Sheriff in full and solid belief that he was helping save our lives for sure, that he was helping keep in office the only true hope we had not to be murdered in our beds once our Negroes got wind of the possibility of change. And Grandpa's story about the hows and whys of the Sheriff's past was not all jigsawed and episodic but rather straight-connected from the start to close. And I heard him tell it many times, but the one I guess that stuck was the summer I left for college, the week cousin Johnny finally had the chance to offer his own version to me all alone in the smoky darkness of his big front porch.

Grandpa was out back in his garden, tying up tomatoes and swatting at the sand fleas that had come up early in the stillness of a mid-August afternoon. We finally sat underneath his favorite fig tree and he poured out two glasses of lemonade and settled back in one of the wooden lawn chairs and sighed.

"You leaving next week?"

"Yes sir. Wednesday."

"Sure about it all?"

"Yes sir. Guess so."

"Good." And he had sighed again and pulled back his hat and wiped at his forehead almost in a single motion. His face looked old, tired and the skin drawn some around his mouth, making him look almost angry in a funny kind of way.

"Election's coming up. Looks like Sheriff has some problems." He had said the words out of nowhere in particular, out maybe from the heart of some deep worry in his head that wouldn't stay put all silent and alone.

"Mr. Robertson running again?"

"Yes. That damn fool's doing it again all right. Talking reform. He's got folks all stirred up. And who knows how them preachers'll deliver the Colored vote this time out. It don't look good at all. Nosir it don't."

Bill Robinson was a renegade Democrat who was altogether too soft on the "Negro question" and suspect on many other counts as well—a white man who didn't much act like one, the old men always said.

"Sheriff's worried, I think."

"Not him, Grandpa. Not worried." The very possibility of worry seemed impossible to me out there in Grandpa's back yard. Out there where everything seemed in place and never changing except for the work the seasons let be done, the garden and the rest, the flowers and maybe the trees if you hadn't noticed them for a while. And the High Sheriff was like that too, more stay-the-same with just a touch of season-change and even that more subtle than the camellia bushes in the far front yard. And worry wasn't never on his face.

"It's all getting different now, Sonny. Different. All un-settled again. I can feel it. Like it was back before he come down here to stay. Like that."

"The Thirties?" It was 1960, but "the Thirties" seemed to me a thing close at hand when Grandpa talked, a nearby time not distant at all but maybe only just as close as the ballpark or the Court House on the shady square. A good walk on a pleasant day with time to tip your hat and talk to friends along the way.

"1932. The year Roos'velt beat that sum-bitch Hoover. 1932." The story always began there and then I'd wander a bit in my thinking and drop back in during World War Two and my birth year of 1941, and then drift off again until it came down to what lay beyond the peace and quiet of the High Sheriff's doing, out there in a Southland readying up to bust open and burn. But this time it was different. The story. Grandpa was giving it out in a way I'd never heard before, his eyes not blinking much and his face at times tilted toward the side as if he were trying to see around the fence post with the red iron rooster mounted on its top out by his watermelon patch.

"It was 1932 and there had been a lynching out in Live Oak and everything was hot and getting hotter. The weath-er. It was August like now. No one knew what set it all off. That was a part of it. Had to be. The heat. But nobody knew what really set it all off—maybe the nigras that robbed that hardware store.

"Maybe it was there before and just not ready yet to cut loose. But the whole nigra situation was not good—not for a long while—young hotheads, most likely from the North, stirring up union talk and such until even the preachers couldn't keep a lid on it all, and then the Ku Klux come back. Like back in the 1920s or maybe they had never gone way but just laid low. Anyways it was hot.

"I was working for the City then. In the tax office and the mayor and sheriff both were scared—"

It went on like that for a while, putting down the groundwork, splashing on some color, getting things ready for the coming of the only law that I had ever known. Details were there thick and plentiful: Ku Klux roving through the city after dark, trucks full of them with their white robes flapping, down through colored town and sometimes getting a stone or bottle tossed at them and setting a few buildings on fire in return and laying on a few beatings here and there until most folks were too scared even to go downtown much less stay down there long enough to shop. Grandpa was taking his time.

"And then the mayor and sheriff run off. Just like that. Cleared out on a Friday and never come back. Nobody knew for sure where they went. Oh there were stories. Yes sir. Plenty of them. But nothing solid or sure. It was a mess. Worse even than before. Judge Conner called for the State Troopers and the Guard, but nothing come of it. The Governor was Ku Klux himself and he just let his own kind take over. Benton Garantoe come in—High Exalted Weezil or whatever in hell he called himself—and sat in the mayor's office. His cousin, Elvin Carter, took over as sheriff and everything really blew up then."

Grandpa sat back in his chair and mopped at his brow again and made his eyes squint like he was in pain. Then he let it all roll on to the finish.

"He come in on the second day. On the railroad. Word was that Judge Conner called on him. Knew him from years back. When he was railroad police or something. Judge got him to come down anyways—somehow—and bring his friends. He had forty or more with him and a machine gun on a wagon and they all moved up from the depot on past Confederate Park real quick and then street by street until they got to the court house and the county jail.

"You could hear the fight all the way down here on Fourteenth Street. Loud. Your Granny wouldn't let me go to work that day—she was scared sick, but I finally did get down there at sunset. And he'd already taken the court house clean and had his men all along the front of the jail and was calling for Elvin and Benton to throw down their guns and surrender. And they did. And all the rest with them. And Mr. Waters began deputizing anybody who'd help him. Even me. Just down there watching. He give me a rifle and set me to guarding a bunch of Ku Klux too drunk to do much else but fall down."

Grandpa sighed; as he brushed at his pants and leaned forward in the chair, his face looked years younger, eyes not nearly as tired and sad as they had been looking and his whole expression confident and strong. It was good to see. His voice was soft and an almost wondering feel to the words come softly out again.

"Me a deputy. For a whole day I was. And then it was back to the tax office and Judge Conner swearing in the new High Sheriff and that started it all, Sonny— that set it all to dancing right down to the here-and-now." And suddenly his face turned back to how it had been at first, tired and older-looking than I had ever seen before, anger there too as he nodded toward the glasses on the table.

"Never even touched that lemonade, Sonny. Must be pretty warm by now."

"Yes sir."

"You be careful down there, y'hear?"

"Yes sir."

"Ain't nobody left no more to do what Sheriff does."

"No sir."

"But you can always come back here." I hadn't engaged him, sipping instead at the tepid lemonade and just for a little while wondering what it felt like to be old and well beyond the need to prove oneself to any living soul.

***

Johnny's story came two days later. The evening I left for school. His house was near the bus depot, and I had already sent my footlocker and a few boxes on ahead. I had an hour or so to wait. He told the story while we rocked in those old cane chairs of his on the big front porch, alone, free from Grandpa and Granny or anybody else who'd keep him from saying much beyond what they'd allow him to say. I had come to say good by.

"You'll get in trouble f'being here."

"I don't care."

"Marcus know about it?"

"No sir. Grandpa's at church. Granny too."

"You'll get in trouble."

"I don't care."

And Johnny began to talk—in the dark of the porch all smoky with his cigarettes and him rocking slowly creak and crack across the close-set boards—words simply tumbling out of nowhere in particular, no connection at times to each other or to any reasonable context except the High Sheriff and his sister and the days back well before Judge Conner called him South.

"Hell-fire—it was her all along. She was his ticket, Sonny. It was her set all the rest of it to going." "She" was the sister, the only sister of the High Sheriff, a woman I had never heard of or seen. She had died a long time ago.

"Red Man weren't nothing when he first come down— back in the early Twenties. Nothing much at all. Except for her. He had her going for him all right and she made it happen." Johnny pulled hard on one of the thickish, hand-rolled cigarettes he made up himself out of some vile-smelling tobacco he bought by the tin for nearly nothing down at Wild's Corner. He drank there too. He drank a lot. I guess he was some kind of cousin to me although I never did get it figured out. The rocker stopped and he turned toward me and suddenly let loose a string of curse words, low and growly and riding down a thick stream of smoke. And then he stopped, leaned back for a second or two and began rocking again as I tried to keep up my end of things.

"Grandpa says…"

"I know what he says. I know that. This here was before all that. Years before. While Sheriff wasn't nothing to
nobody. It was her that made all the rest happen for him.
She was his ticket off the railroad. She done it all." And he
described her in the greatest detail—from her red hair, long
and thick and full of some kind of smell he never could
make come exactly clear—from all that right down past her
face—eyes green and lips all peach-colored and cheeks
rouged up and skin full of freckles and so white in between
that it made you think of cream all pure and smooth—and
on down further to her neck and shoulders, delicate-like
and her tits (he said that) just kept on rolling out forever
when she let him help her get on down to business by taking off her clothes a piece at a time until the best part (he
called it that—the "best part") come free and ready for most
anything but a straight-on fucking (he had liked that word
the most and right through our time on the porch sometimes whole sentences had come out with nothing but it
there all alone and strong, and then he'd laugh and laugh
and suck in so much smoke that I had thought he'd just
never get a decent breath again).

"Yes sir, she let me do ever-damned-thing, Sonny. Everthing. Except fuck her. She never did let me do that."

"But why?"

"Why?"

"Yes sir." It had all seemed—after a few straight
minutes—something like one of the stories in the books Bill
Mason and me had found back when we were maybe elev-
en or twelve down in that old barn near the railroad depot.
Stories about whores and good women who had gone bad
and pictures in among the stories that showed it all and

more than I had ever even thought about as being part of
what I'd come upon when I got finally grown. The pictures
had made my belly feel funny and the stories kept on coming back to mind and it had felt and sounded like that as
Johnny's voice got low and lower and Sheriff's sister got a
name, Malinda, and Sheriff himself started coming in like
nothing I had ever heard before.

"He come down here from Georgia all right, Sonny.
From Slackbridge. An' nobody knows why he come down.
Not that first time anyways. Nobody. Some says one thing.
Some says another. But you know what I think?" Johnny
had stopped rocking then and put out a bare trace of a cigarette in one of the plant pots and lit another one almost in
the same motion.

"No sir." I had leaned in closer. Johnny smelled like
he'd stepped in dog crap.

"He knowed she wasn't clean. An' they'd found it out
up there in Slackbridge, y'see, so he just used the railroad
and come on down here where nobody knew nothing."

"Not clean?"

"An' he didn't do much to get her well neither. Just
enough so's you'd never know. So's it most times wouldn't
rub off. Something. He had others too."

"Sisters?"

"No—God no—only the one. Other girls. High-yellers.
A few white trash. Good lookers. Real good lookers. All sick
too, I think. One way or another. Fixed up to pass but never
all the way well. 'Course he dropped 'em if they did get
caught—and never got caught himself neither. Yessir. He

had lots of girls. An' he used them up. Ever one. To get in good with the right people. Get in good and solid with them folks most of all. But her he used the worst of all. Yes sir he did."

"Malinda?"

"Yeah. She was somethin'." And he stopped rocking and let out a thick stream of smoke and shifted around in the chair. The dog crap smell got stronger as he began to giggle and snort like he had just heard a powerful joke from out there somewhere in the dark of the front yard. Crickets began to sound and tree frogs too and it all got mixed together and I got up to leave. And then he stopped giggling and began to rock again, the tip of his cigarette bright glowing as I felt for the screen door latch—and fingered the bus ticket in my pocket—and rested for a little while among the creak and slap and cricket-chirr and tree frog clatter, with both the stories there like feathered smoke down in the darkness of my own trip south.

-2-

"Patriots at Sunset"

It was a coolish, late afternoon, December, Christmas break and I was coming home for the first time since school started back in August. I had just bought a near wreck of a car from my roommate and was trying it out. I had taken a shortcut, but the St. Cristobel County line seemed clogged as I sat waiting in a mess of cars that stretched back single-file at least five miles toward the southeast. The radio didn't work and I had finished my last cigarette an hour ago while passing through Waldo. I turned off the engine and drummed my fingers on the steering wheel and then decided to get out and see what the trouble was up ahead.

"Hoped I'd miss it this time out—take a full damn hour t'get past all this here—" The red-faced man in the car just ahead spoke out of one side of his mouth, a thick and soggy stub of a cigar stuck in the corner of the other. He was resting against the driver's side and kicking at something, a bright rock or balled up candy wrapper, down near the front door of his car. No traffic was coming in the opposite direction. "Where you headed, son?"

"St. Cristobel."

"I'm heading for the beach. Take me a full damn hour to pass, I bet. Look out—" He motioned up ahead at some cars in the opposite lane that suddenly were beginning to come on, and then he stepped to the front of his car. I followed. "Maybe not—here come a few at least. Our turn soon. Maybe it won't take too long now. I sure hope not."

"What's up there?"

"Been like this for at least two months now. Mostly on Fridays. I couldn't avoid 'er this time. Sales convention in Starke. Just let out s'afternoon. Damn."

I walked onto the shoulder of the road and tried to make out what was going on, but it was too far away and other drivers were walking through the tall grass all up along the line.

"You live in St. Cristobel long, son?" The red-faced man had gotten rid of the cigar and was rubbing at the back of his neck with a bright blue handkerchief. His shirt was sweat- stained and his black suspenders looked too short, pulling hard at his shiny pants and making his dull white socks show nearly all the way to his calfs.

"All my life. Born and raised."

"I'm from the Beach myself. Damn. Lookit them cars go. Must be double-teamin' up there t'get 'em going that fast. Damn." He walked back to the edge of the road, wiping at his face again and staring at the cars rolling by. One driver's face was bloody and his car full of squalling kids.

"What's that—wreck?"

"Jesus H.—must've mouthed off—damn." He stepped quickly back from the road and moved close to me. His face was covered in beads of sweat even though a cool breeze had come up from the nearby woods. "I bet it's the Live Oak crew this time. That was a white man in that car. You see him? Shit. That don't look good at all."

"Who's up there?"

The man coughed and spat straight at a clump of brown grass that spilled out onto the road near his car.

"Ku Klux. Damn Live Oak Coonhunters, I bet. You see that white man? You saw that, right?"

"Yes." His face had been nearly covered in blood and the kids had made a sound like puppies being stepped on hard.

"Damn fool mouthed off. Refused to pay. Whatever. One reason's good as another. Jesus H., son—hope you got some money on you."

***

Back in my car, barely moving, a rush of black smoke boiling on up ahead and a five dollar bill in my shirt pocket, last of my job money from school (delivering sandwiches to the dorms and frat houses), nothing in my wallet and just enough gas to get through this I hoped and the last run on to home. The red-faced man had filled me in—just before our line of traffic jolted to life:

"See—you gotta pay 'em something."

"Why?"

"Who knows? Something different every time. White Defense Fund last time I got caught. White Schools Book Fund time before that. One time it was just buckets pushed in your face and no reason given. And them Live Oak boys're the worst. Shit. Just pay up an' don't say nothing."

The cars were moving a bit faster, the sun below the tallest pines and a deep red there blending into a more golden and shadow-streaked sweep along the grass and palmetto to either side of the road. It was late. I wished the radio worked. The car ahead, the red-faced man, suddenly signaled, a fat arm flapping out, and then his car slowly pulled off the road onto a bare spot of gravel near a ruined plank fence that almost encircled a small graveyard. He looked sick as I passed, and I yelled out to see if he needed help but he waved me on impatiently as if I were an unexpected interruption in an otherwise well-planned afternoon. Glancing back, I saw that he had another cigar in his mouth and was twisting the cap off a pint bottle. My car was nearly to the boil of black smoke before I decided to hide the bill deep in my pants pocket. The road took a turn toward the east, away from the sun and curved a bit on among the streaks of shadow and moving, golden light. I wasn't planning on giving them a dime.

"Hey there, white man. What you got for us here?"

The voice came slightly muffled through a shiny red hood, slit holes showing two bright blue eyes just as the sun began to drop behind a large oak out in a plowed field. The eyes looked kindly. He was shaking a big white bucket that was filled with mostly paper money.

"I—I—" Other hoods were bobbing up and down both sides of the road and a fire was roaring flames at least ten feet into the air in a washed out place of sand and coquina beside a palmetto thicket. Two carloads of Negroes were parked near the fire and a knot of white hoods was there as well, some cradling shotguns in their arms and a few others holding baseball bats.

"You got something for the cause, I bet. Here you go—put 'er right in here." A few white hoods pulled open one of the car doors and jerked the driver outside. He was a heavyset Negro, baldheaded and dressed in a red shirt and baggy tan pants. A sheriff's car rolled up just then, followed by three more—lights flashing and making me relax almost at once.

"I—I'm a student—"

"Do what?"

"I'm a student."

"Well now that's fine, son—but we ain't got no student rate here. Y'see?" He had laughed, deep and gargle-like,

the force of it all pushing the hood up and down and showing a little bit of shirt color, a blue collar with police insignia,
St. Cristobel City Police clearly there all shiny and clean.

"I don't have—"

"Much money? Hell, son—I know how that goes, but
we in a war here an' we need ever damn dime we can get.
See?"

The Negro was on the ground and the white hoods
gathered around and began kicking him, not particularly
hard but almost casually, like what you'd do to a dirt clod or
acorn on the sidewalk. The sheriff's deputies were watching
and a few lit up cigarettes and began to direct traffic to free
up the bucket brigade in the opposite lane. The red hood
had been talking apparently all along.

"...so you gotta choose, son—them or us. Ain't no other way. Them or us. Apes or white men like me and you.
Y'see?"

The voice was low, kindly, an oldish quality there, almost reassuring, a pleading there down in it too that made
me think for just a second of the way my Grandpa sounded
late at night and deep within a tale of how things used to
be—of how we every one had been all lost and nearly ruined until Red-Man Waters had come to tame the white
hoods and the coloreds both—and how we all were safe
because of what he did. And then I saw the man himself—
striding in the deep grass with four deputies behind him, tall
still and yet heavier than when I last had seen him, a big
white Stetson bobbing on his head and everybody walking
right up to where the fallen Negro groaned and held his
head in both hands while little children cried from some-

where lost to sight. The High Sheriff stopped, turned his back on the Negro, and faced full into the last of the sunlight, the whole scene lit up for just a second or two and then lost to shadow-streak, faded into near darkness right before the second Negro got pulled out from his car and all of it began again.

I found the five dollar bill on the fourth try, digging deep into my pockets, my fingers shaking and cold and closing on it finally and a feeling of gratefulness spreading out all down inside me as I handed it over to the kindly eyes and got waved free to go on home.

-3-

"Solemnity"

The tree was perfect. Had been so for generations. It had limbs thick and strong and just the right distance from the ground: a giant oak—old and tested and sure and grounded solid in the deep woods where it had stood since even before the first written records of its use: Nigger Oak.

Ten was the proper number for the work. Ten men could always do it right. And ten had gathered that evening at Jameson's Barber Shop—in the big back room after Bret Jameson locked the front door and drew down the shop window shades. Bret led the rest—the three Lewis Brothers, Cal Morris, Sam Willis, Parker Dobbs, Earl Samford and Billy Smith and me. Bret had been leader a long, long time. And he had done all the talking.

"We got that jig a'ready. Boys over at Chaseville got him last night. All set to go." Nothing more had to be said after that. And the ride to Nigger Oak was silent too. Except for the sometimes sniffling and crying of the jig all tied up between Earl Samford and me in the backseat of the middle car. He smelled like kerosene and cooked greens. He got pretty quiet by the time we quit driving. The car headlights made a bright, bug-caught circle of light around the tree.

"Get 'im on out here, boys." Bret was bareheaded; we were too. But dressed in our best robes. Silk. Like it had been done since the late thirties. High Sheriff Waters would have been proud as the rope sailed up and slid quick and smooth over the second lowest limb. One of the Lewis brothers held the noose. The jig was a high-yeller with a pie-shaped face. He had done something bad. But nobody had to know just what. That had all been settled way back up the line.

"Get 'im over there." The jig was gagged with a thick piece of shiny cloth. His eyes rolled and he slumped once or twice, shuffling his feet and moaning in that funny kind of way they always do. Billy Smith laughed and Bret snapped around and almost growled him into the right kind of quiet. Bret always got in the first blow. This time a knee jab mid-groin that brought the jig down to his knees. Then Bret held his arms in turn for everybody else to get a chance. Like always. Tree frogs clattered overhead and from down deeper in the Ponsell Woods some kind of nightbird screeched a few times and got lost in a rising up of cricket chirr closer at hand.

The jig only groaned a little more as he began his dancing up above the white sand, in among the bugs that fluttered more and more in the headlights of the cars, a heel-and-toe in air, eyes popping now and everything in order all around.

It was a perfect night.

After Hours with the Wolfman

Hannah Roche felt the weight of each one of her sixty years as she tugged at the stiff collar of her long, black cape and leaned on the curved end of the bar. Her red-tipped, plastic fangs rested near a pool of beer and the remains of a roast beef sandwich and the elbow of a nearly drunk werewolf who had tried all evening to reach a paw through the black lace front of her gown. As she poured herself a fresh ginger-ale, she noticed that he seemed to be thinking of trying it again, his left paw flopping up and down on the bar like it wanted to fly. The Halloween party was finally over and all she wanted to do was lock up the Kawli-ga Klub and drive home and get into a bathtub full of warm water and bubbles.

"C'mon, Jack—drink up. Closing time." She couldn't figure out who was inside the werewolf, his costume so complete that nothing much of his natural body was left uncovered, with furry paws and claws so life-like that he had seemed ready to drop down on all fours and rush out the front door to howl and bite and slash out at whoever he could find. "C'mon—hey—can't you hear me?" His slightly flattened face was now pointed away from her, toward the row of draft handles midway down the bar. His head hadn't moved in almost ten minutes. "Hey—drink up, I said." She nudged his elbow and looked to see if Buck, her regular barman, had come back from the storeroom.

"Whazzit?" The werewolf grunted and turned his face toward hers, mouth still fixed in the same sharp-toothed near grin that was there when he came in and howled a few times and ordered his first beer. "Gimme 'nother beer." The eyes showing through the fur-edged holes in the mask were almost totally red, moist-looking as if circles of film or tinted glass had been put there to further obscure the exact characteristics of the head inside. Buck was helping a few devils and a badly weaving hunchback out the front door. The werewolf clicked with the tips of his claws at a half-empty glass.

"Drink what you got—party's over." All the others had gone—finally—and the room was smoke-choked and too warm, and its center was streaked in the black and orange remnants of bunting—plastic skeletons dangling from the ceiling around the dance floor and posters of witches and arch-backed black cats covering portions of the walls and the big screen to the left of the curved bar trying to show a medley of video horror rock that had begun the first ugliest man contest nearly four hours ago and made the werewolf howl.

"Gimme 'nother beer, I said." His eyebrows bushed out and down, making the red of the peephole eyes darker each time he moved his head. "C'mon, Hannah—one more—" The voice went up a notch, for the first time since he had come in, losing the huskiness which had made her grow more and more uneasy the longer he stayed at the bar. The way he said her name sounded familiar. He had won ugliest man and best costume and nobody had guessed who he was.

"Need anything, Hannah?" Buck stood to one side of a fluttering Dracula poster and made a jerking motion toward the bar with his thumb. She started to nod "yes" but something in the way the werewolf tensed his shoulders and cocked his head made her stop.

"No—but make sure nobody passed out in the can." The werewolf seemed to relax as he picked up the glass with both paws, claws curling about the rim and some of the beer spilling down over his chin whiskers as he drank it off.

"You want anything done about all this here?" Buck swept a hand in the air out toward the chaos behind him and yawned.

"No—we'll clean up tomorrow—go on home."

"C'mon—'nother beer, Hannah—jus' th'one more an' thas it—huh?" His elbows slipped off the bar and in catching his balance, a flash of bare skin showed where the mask met the top of his shoulders. "Jus' th'one?"

"Look," she unsnapped her cape and draped it over one of the barstools, "it's past time. Why don't you go on home an' get some sleep? Let me call you a cab." He had made his first grab, a lurching grope that nearly ripped out the top of her dress, just minutes after he downed his third beer. Buck had threatened to throw him out then but two identically-wrapped mummies had gotten into a fist fight over near the pool tables and Hannah let it ride. After that, the grabs had gotten less accurate.

"Gimme 'nother beer an' I'll tell you who I am." He somehow made his eyebrows go up and down, nose seeming to flare a bit from the motion. "You ain't got no idea—right? Right?"

"Right."

"See? You ain't got no idea. C'mon—ast me who I am. Ast." He leaned on the bar and folded his paws near the half-eaten sandwich.

"Ok—who are you?" She came around and sat on a barstool just out of reach. The voice was becoming more and more familiar, a certain catch to it that she had heard before. She wondered if Buck had left his shotgun under the bar.

"Guess." The mask slipped, eyeholes briefly titling and then settling back into place.

"I ain't got time for this, Jack—so why don't you get your—"

"No—wrong! W-r-o-n-g. Not Jack. I ain't Jack." The laugh didn't match the voice, giggle-like and sounding as if it might not be able to stop without help.

"Look," she slid down from the stool and walked back around the bar, "I done told you I ain't got time for none of this—so get it in gear and get on down the road." In the dim light from a nearby beer sign, she could just make out the polished stock of the shotgun and beside it her own tape-wrapped baseball bat. She wanted to go home and wash all the green paint off her face. The party had not gone well, not even half the Saturday night regulars showing up, most of them without costumes and already well on the way to unconsciousness. And somebody had messed up the big screen, like now mostly playing and replaying the same gory segment of some horror-rock DVD until even the early drunks began to notice. She picked up the remote and clicked the screen dark just as the decapitation of a group of living Raggedy Ann dolls began showing for at least the tenth time. The werewolf raised his paws to his lips as if he were biting his claws. He looked as if he was trying to be cute, making his nose scrunch up as he moved his head. "Ok—Ok, are you Governor Hargrave?"

"No! Noooo. N-O. God no." The head bobbed up and down as he let the paws drop onto the bar, claws clicking out loudly and a gurgling sound coming out of the mouth. "I ain't no nigger, for Godssake." He shifted his weight on the stool and cocked his head again, this time reminding Hannah of a fuzzy puppy. "You got one more guess."

"Pluto." She leaned back against the mirror beside the cash register and crossed her ankles, enjoying the way he held his sides as he laughed, making an almost gasping sound like he was sucking in too much air.

"Pluto! God—Pluto? C'mon Hannah. Pluto?" He suddenly pulled up on his ears and slipped the mask free, holding it above his head while red hair frizzed out in all directions and a mist of sweat fanned down onto the bar. "It's me—m-e," he dropped the mask, and rested his arms on top, bending the ears and making both the nose and mouth bulge, rubber teeth sticking out in several different directions.

"Riley?" The eyes made her jump, red dots that poked out from the swollen flesh surrounding them like tiny embers somehow stuck down to burn themselves out in a snow bank. "What happened to your face?" At a glance, it was hard to tell it was Riley Dribbet, even his hair seeming different, coarser and slicked down in a few places. She hadn't seen him since he went south to buy guns. At least that's what she was told. Over a year ago. Gone south from sawmill work and janitoring at the high school. Nothing was ever certain about Riley, though. Nothing. "You look like you been beat up."

"Huh?" He pushed the mask to one side and leaned over to see himself in the mirror. "I dunno—somethin' I ate maybe. They got funny food down where I been, Hannah. I jus' got back. Yet'day, I think."

"Where've you been? Mexico?"

"Yeah—an' other places too." He patted at the head and smiled. "C'mon—you knew it was me all 'long—right?"

"You had me going." She moved back closer to the bar, trying to make this version of Riley fit in with the one she had known since he was a child, but the bobbing head and sweat-soaked hair and ears and a nose that seemed pushed in on themselves made it almost impossible. His father had been her first, over forty years now gone by since the week before her sixteenth birthday, steel ribs in the bed of an old truck pressing hard into her back even through a pallet and a nasty-smelling quilt and John Paul making a snorting noise through his nose as he poked into her, painfully, one hand holding the side of the truck.

--don't cry—it's—good—don't, Hannah—I love you Hannah—

She had thought she was bleeding to death by the time John Paul had let her go home, his voice distant-sounding and the house lights blinking by in the nighttime like giant fire flies resting up between flights.

—c'mon, Hannah—it—was—good—I love you girl—

Riley rubbed a paw over a pool of beer and tried to smile, but his cheeks now seemed frozen, skin not giving much around the lips and his eyes blinking too rapidly as he gave it up and sucked in some air over his clenched teeth. The costume contrasted sharply with his hair. He looked nothing like John Paul.

"Where'd you get something like that, Riley?"

"Place down in Juarez sells 'em. Last one of these they had though." The smile tried to come back. "Good party, Hannah." His voice was sounding steadier. "How 'bout that beer?"

"You've had enough." Several lines of sweat began to run down her back, beneath the new black slip that she had struggled into at the house, her skin now feeling almost basted with a moisture that seemed to be making her hotter the longer Riley's head bobbed and his eyes blinked. "I got to close up." The Halloween party had not helped, almost from the first seeming less like a celebration than a gathering of desperately frightened people, fewer even in number than on a regular Saturday night, blood-spattered costumes that after a while whirled and jerked to no particular rhythm, dancing alone or sometimes with another as if by accident, keeping clear of any real contact or conversation longer than was necessary to get another drink or order a sandwich. And the band Buck had helped her hire had played so badly that two Grim Reapers attacked the chicken-wire stage shield with their plastic scythes.

"You should seen Stanton's place, Hannah." He reached for the mask and began picking at the ears with one of his claws. "Had 'em lined up clear out to th'pumps."

"That museum of his?" She tried to picture what it might look like on the inside, behind and beneath the flashing billboards and hand-lettered signs that Stanton had been putting up on the roof and sides of the old Trading Post in stages for over two months until the old cabin no longer even had the same shape it had back when she worked there after school. "Stanton open it already?"

"Tonight. Big party, Hannah. Free beer and peanuts, y'know?"

"Yeah." She noticed that Buck had shut down the outside lights, windows along the far wall no longer flashing bright orange but now reflecting the beer signs above the bar. The room was almost dark. "I know he's crazy."

"But he got hisself some kind a place goin' over there buddies. Yessir, he does." The mask was on its side, red eyes fixed on the sandwich and the nearly empty shelves beyond, big front teeth coming together each time Riley tapped down on it with the flat of his paw. "Costez two dollars just to get in." He licked his lips and tried the smile again. "Where you 'supose he got all that stuff?"

"I don't know. What's he got?" She never could picture Stanton in the Trading Post, behind the long counter set up higher than the main room and stretching nearly the length of one of the walls, with the candy bowl pyramids and jars of honey and folded quilts and the tourists all talking at once or sitting quietly in the rough, wooden booths sipping lemonade or eating homemade ice-cream in the summer-time and hot chocolate and ham biscuits in the fall. She had worked there all through high school and for years after-wards, saving the money that together with what she man-aged to salvage from the sale of her parents' house and land had made it possible for her to buy the Kawliga Klub over twenty years ago. Stanton always reminded her of a coon, dark circles around his eyes and hands that never stopped moving the few times he had stopped in for a beer.

"You ought go see, Hannah." Riley's face looked red, eyes nearly glazed over and watery, reminding her of his daddy's and taking her back in spite of herself once more to that first night and the others when she had gasped and grunted under a man who never stopped saying he loved her. But he hadn't quite made it legal, finally marrying a girl from Atlanta and leaving Hannah with nobody much but Buck and sometimes a salesman or a soldier set free on a weekend pass. The girl from Atlanta had lost three babies and then died giving Riley to a John Paul who from the first had wanted little to do with him, leaving the boy to grow up as best he could. To Hannah, Riley had never seemed quite right, something about the way he smiled making her uncomfortable, causing her skin to tingle in an almost pain-ful way. And his father's death and Vietnam had made eve-rything worse.

"It's somethin' a'right, Hannah. He even got these Jew heads in there."

"What?" His words didn't sound right, slurred, swal-lowed, the last ones coming down muffled in phlegm. She rubbed a hand across the top of her breasts, the wet there feeling sticky, the tips of her fingers seeming to come away coated with whatever it was they put in the vampire makeup she had smoothed on for the party. "What'd you say?"

"Anyways I think that's what he called 'em. Lil' black hairy things." The smile finally made it, teeth showing yellowish and chipped in front. "That costed a dollar extra."

"What did?" She wished Riley had not decided to join her party, had decided instead to stay among whatever it was that Stanton had done to the old Trading Post. She noticed that the more he talked, the more her stomach rolled and constricted, making even the skin across her pelvis feel stretched tight to the point of pain. His eyes seemed just before laughing.

"The Nazi Room." He smacked his lips and ran his tongue over the lower one. "Got this great big picture of Hitler in there. Glass cases full of stuff." He scratched at his nose with a slightly bent claw and slid down off the stool. "Had some good beer too—whole keg of it over by the door." He coughed. "'Course I liked the Klan Heroes better. Most of my boys in the Rangers did too. Had J.B. Stoner's shotgun and pistol in there. Flags. Crosses. Robert Shelton's hood. Connie Lynch's shoes. All kinds of stuff."

"And Jew heads?" She thought of the movies she had seen on TV, stick-figure bodies being bulldozed into deep pits and skulls piled on top of each other like pineapples in a supermarket.

"What?"

"Jew heads. You said, Jew heads." His father had pro-posed to her there in the ice-cream parlor just off the moun-tain craft aisles, the years since making the scene itself seem fuzzy, somehow unreal and rigid, the words he spoke not strong enough to come back by themselves, needing an effort beyond what she cared to put out so late at night. The girl from Atlanta hadn't been dead but a week.

"Hoods, Hannah. Musta had ten of 'em. Robert Shel-ton's. Glen Miller's. David Duke's. Even Bubba Tugman's. You remember Bubba, don't you, Hannah? Lived over near Craig's Corners. The ol' boy the Feds come down on back after that third church bombing?"

"No. The Jew heads." Her gown felt too tight, constrict-ing across her stomach and hips.

"Jew heads? Oh yeah—Jew heads—carvings. Some kind a soap." He reached for the mask and tucked it under his arm, eyeholes pointed toward Hannah and the ears curved out toward the sides like fat antennae. "You ain't gonna give me no beer?"

"You get on home, Riley. Get some sleep." She un-hooked the back of her gown and rubbed at her neck. Her fingers felt stiff. "Cost extra to see them?"

"The Jew Heads?" He moved toward the front door, stepping carefully into the near darkness beyond the bar lights.

"Yes." John Paul had stood by the ice-cream churn and shuffled his feet, making her feel like some mother who had just caught her son stealing cookies. Riley had been a week old.

"Yeah—extra—had to put your dollar in this helmet."

"Was it worth it?" She decided against a bath. A warm shower would feel better. John Paul never asked again.

"Well—I think he might of lost money on the beer."

The Flagellant Next Door

The flagellant next door was sitting on the back steps of the duplex, sipping at a tall, miniature umbrella-topped drink, perhaps a gin or vodka-something in a glass as green as a spring frog's wet feet. He, the flagellant, was sleepy and didn't bother to shoo away the flies that came gratefully to rest in the bloody mess of his back and in the steady rivulets that streaked his chest in three separate places. He sipped and yawned and seemed not to notice Hector Silverthorpe come in from a hard day's guarding of the crematoria over in Death Camp II. Hector was a professional Holocaust re-enactor, a Ukrainian Hiwi this month, looking forward to a different role when the next auditions came along in about six months. The flagellant sipped long and sighed and let the flies have their way. Hector made it past him and through the back door of his own apartment and into the freshly painted kitchen.

It had been a long day, Thursday, Children's Transport Day, with many visitors (at $10.00 a head and no exceptions) and brats to kill in three shows since nine o'clock that morning. The brats all had mothers and all had naptime built into their contracts, which spread out the shows at least two hours beyond what was usual. The camp was one of three in Georgia, financed by the Jack Onan Ministries, Inc. as Christian "apologies" (the pamphlets said), as Christian "sorrow " and "love" for the "People of the Book—so sorely used." Hector rested his machine gun against the wall beside the door and unbuttoned his tunic. The flagellant had started in again—a whoosh and slap of whip and an almost cadenced moaning coming in clear and strong as Hector opened the fridge and found he had no beer.

***

Hector woke up in a sweat and shivering from some dream that wouldn't properly stay beyond the turning on of the bedside lamp and the pound pound pound and the rattle and crash of the glass in the front door. He hurried to the living room and looked through a splintered but open jalousie and saw the flagellant there—bowed beneath a crude wooden cross and using the top to make the front door shake.

"Hey—hey you stop!" Hector pushed open the door and the flagellant fell down to his knees—the cross now upright behind his back and the top swaying gently above his bowed and thorn-crowned, bloodied head.

"I thirst!" The flagellant raised his head and looked straight at Hector, eyes rolling up and lips crusted with blood that his tongue was busy licking. For some reason, there were no flies. "I thirst!" His mouth formed a jagged smear across his face.

"There is no beer." Hector yawned. "And it's too late to buy more." He yawned again and scratched at his side. "You'll have to come back."

"When?" The flagellant shifted the cross and slowly rose from his knees.

"Tomorrow—today–daylight—the afternoon." Hector was tired. Tomorrow—today was a holiday.

"Not until then?"

"Yes."

"But it's Good Friday."

"Oh. Right. Sorry. Busy day for you. I forgot."

"And then I'll be in the tomb sleeping."

"Yes. I know, I know. How about Sunday then? How's that?"

"Yes. Sunday. Sunday is good. Yes." And he staggered and fell and got up and fell again and finally made it to his side of the yard.

Hector went back to sleep.

***

Saturday was loud. Pulling up the bedroom blinds, Hector rubbed his eyes and scanned the backyard. An amplified bluegrass band had decided to practice under the old oak behind the duplex, in one of the neighboring yards but close enough to wake up the flagellant well before the BIG DAY. Hector saw him nearly fall off the back deck, wrapped in what looked to be bright white terry cloth, oozing just a bit and chased by a generous swarm of flies. The bluegrass band stopped and then began again, loud-pumped into a ragged chasing after something like "Ain't

No Grave"—the instruments not quite together at the first but nearly there just when the lead voice came in strong—a skinny, red- haired mandolin picker singing high and sweet as the flagellant hopped, feet and legs caught up in unravelling terry cloth, through the tall grass near the duplex side of the tree.

> *Go down yonder, Gabriel--*
> *Put your foot on the land and sea—*

The flagellant was trying to yell something, hopping in a dance-like sway from side to side, making those noises that he sometimes made when he forgot where he had put his favorite whip—a strong and wavering shriek of almost-words that jerked along in a way that didn't quite seem tied to anything that even made it close to real.

"eyyyyyyyyyy—uh-uh—eyyyyyyyyy—uh—uhhhhhh—eyyyyyyy—"

Hector hated it when he did that. But the redhead and the band hadn't noticed anything at all.

> *Don't blow your trumpet, boy*
> *Until you hear from me—*
> *There ain't no grave—gonna hold my body*
> *down—*

Hector sat down on the edge of the bed to watch. It was nearly noon and the flagellant hop-danced through a strong sunlight that made his terry cloth binding sparkle as it caught the tops of the tall grass.

"eyyyyyyyyyyyyy—uhhhhhhh—eyyyyy—nooooooo—"

The redhead leaned into the mike and held a high note on the "grave" that made the glass in the window rattle a little bit. The flagellant began to hop harder, red-splotched terry cloth now flapping out his sides like dying wings, and his voice become an even match with the band, loud and louder with each wing-flap and grass-caught swirl of cloth.

"noooooooo—nooooooo—noooooooooo—"

> *Ain't no grave can hold my body*
> *down—*
> *When I hear that trumpet sound—*

"eyyyyyyyyy—eyyyyyyyyy—noooooo—eyyyyy—"

> *Gonna get up out the ground—*
> *There ain't no grave—gonna hold—*

The flagellant finally won—voice a bellow like a bull caught hard by pain, words now clear and whole and covering up the music that had finally noticed he was there.

"Saturday—Saturday—Saturday—Saturday—"

The redhead pushed the mike away and someone must have bumped into a speaker because it all sounded like static for the few seconds it took the flagellant to make it up under the tree. But then the speakers came in again, picking up the conversation and clear even through the closed windows of Hector's bedroom.

"Saturday—it's not time yet—Saturday—"

"Yes sir, it's Saturday all right. Yes sir."

The redhead had a low, raspy, funny voice—slow and careful with his words. The others put down their instruments and pushed in around the flagellant, blocking Hector's view. The sound was strong, though—clear and like they all were just outside the window.

"It's not time."

"We don't know that for sure, Cap'n. No sir, we don't. You don't look too good to me. What's wrong? You been in a accident?"

"What?"

"You need he'p, looks like."

"No. No help—I need to wait—to wait—"

"Call him some he'p, Billy—St. Gadarene's the clostest, I think. That's a good place to go. Yes sir, it is."

"No—no I can't do that—I—I—"

The band helped the flagellant to sit down on the edge of the tall grass, gently so, with the redhead slinging his mandolin over his shoulder and trying to tug and pat all the bloody cloth back into place. The microphone picked up only a few words now, the voices coming in and out and static rising up again an occasional whistle and pop within a crackling roar.

"—time—not—"

"—help—soon—"

"—lost—gone—"

The ambulance had blue thunderbolts down its sides. Hector yawned and wondered who would get the apartment next door now that Eastertide had come.

We Don't Do Dips Anymore

I think I first noticed it during a gubernatorial debate. Evelyn (my wife of twenty years) was entertaining her precinct workers in the game room and I was passing through, mingling slowly through her guests on my way to the pool out back and my other liquor cabinet, the one inside the storage shed that no one knew about but me and Charlie Rourke, the Irish plumber. Evelyn was big on politics in those days which made for a lot of strangers in our home. And candidates as well. Even a few national ones, I think. But all liberals and losers every one. Now I've never even registered to vote myself, but if I ever did I'd not waste my time voting for a liberal. No sir I wouldn't. No. Not even the way things have turned out. But anyway, back then the TV screen was full of the latest liberal's face when I came in, a clean-looking face all tanned with teeth in it like polished ivory used to look back when you could still buy the damned stuff over the counter. The liberal that particular day was Peter Caldwell, Jr.—dreamer (a book: *The Challenge of Love*), family man (four bright-eyed boy/girls and a wife so thin she seemed to disappear each time she turned to wave at someone in a crowd), veteran (Coast Guard Reserve), and four-term mayor (I think) of Little Floridian or some such place down somewhere in the center of the state. So the Florida Liberals' current hope was Peter Caldwell, Jr. and the people in my home were all a-twitter over every word he mumbled through those nearly perfect teeth. And I (Robert C. Potter) was mingling slowly toward the door.

"Isn't he just the best-looking thing you ever saw?"

I don't remember who it was who spoke but the sentence stuck, has stuck for some time now, well beyond the liberal's defeat and teary mumbles at the victory-wake my wife set up election night. I don't know *why* it stuck except it came out at the very second that I looked down at the catered feast all multi-colored (hot and cold) packed tight upon our biggest table and on rolling carts along the wall and saw not one thing there that even seemed remotely like a dip. No dip at all. And *that* (I know and now so clear) was somehow what it must have been that set the rest in motion. The changes and the changing, the nothing firm in place or steady to the eye or hand or foot, not anything left as it was or should have been. All moving—everything in motion even as I watched it go and even as I came too late to see it one last time. And of the beginning only the voice remains:

"Isn't he just the best-looking thing you ever saw?" Shrill-feminine and then the deeper raspy answer from my wife that night as we got into bed beneath a quilt and sheets I'd never seen before:

"Oh we don't do dips anymore."

She smiled, I think, a little quick one as she plumped a funny-colored pillow up against the headboard and then dropped down on her side. I sat there in pajamas only barely familiar, feet beside a pair of leather slippers almost like the ones I used to wear. The room itself looked freshly papered and my voice had sounded distant when I finally spoke again, seeming far away from where I clearly was, like something moving in and out of range.

"Not at all? No dips at all?"

"No. No one does dips. Are you all right, Robert?"

"What?"

"You sound—well—strange. Indigestion again?"

"How long have they been gone?"

"What did you say?"

"The dips—how long have—"

"Would a warm glass of milk help, dear?"

"No—you see, I just noticed—I—have you re-papered this room?"

"The room?"

"Yes—*here*—have you re-papered it? It looks like—"

"Last week. Yes. Don't you remember? You chose the design yourself."

"I did?"

"Yes. 'Highland Fantasy.' Remember?"

"No."

"Peter looked good this evening, don't you think?"

"'Highland Fantasy'?"

"He sounded better too—not so—well—stiff and mumbly—"

"Are you coming to Sunday school tomorrow?"

"What did you say, Robert?"

"Sunday School—tomorrow *is* Sunday, isn't it?"

"Yes—yes it is but I don't see what—"

"Well? Are you coming to Sunday school or not?"

"But, Robert—we don't attend Sunday school. Or church, for that matter. Are you sure I can't get you something for your stomach? Some flat cola maybe or—"

"What do you mean we don't attend—I—I've been a Methodist all my life—and—I—I *teach* the young adults for godssake—I—then you're not coming? Is that what you're trying to say? Well? Is it?"

"Let's try to get some sleep, dear. It's been a long, tiring day. Let's just try to—"

"No! Dammit Evelyn—are you coming or not?"

"Where, dear?"

"To church goddammit—to Sunday school *and* church—or just to Sunday School or just to church—or—or—are you staying home—or—"

"But we don't *attend* church any more, Robert."

"Why do you keep saying that? If you don't want to come just—"

"Not for ten years now. Not since you discovered the hypocrites there. And the frauds. The—what did you used to call them? Oh—what *was* that word?"

"We don't attend church?"

"That's right, dear. Don't you think Governor Bocks treated Peter with more respect than in that other debate? Did you notice how polite he was?"

"I—I—"

"Florida really needs him."

"Bocks?"

"No, silly—*Peter*. Are you OK now?"

"Yes. You're—you're sure about the dips?"

"Oh *Robert*—come to bed!"

And I did. Every night for a month and every night I swear beneath a slightly different quilt and sheets that seemed to change their color with the time of day. I own an exterminating company (BUG BLASTERS) and took an early semi-retirement last year, so most days I've been home at lunch or afternoons to swim in the pool or drink a gin or two with Charlie Rourke when something calls him out to work nearby. My own plumbing is in excellent shape. Charlie did it new five years ago and so far not spigot, pipe or sink has changed its shape or color. Not like the sheets and quilt and paper on the walls and all the rest of it—the church I couldn't find and no dip anywhere in town. I tried to bring it up to Charlie early on, right after I misplaced my car.

"But dammit, Charlie—it was *never* blue!"

"OK OK—you oughta *know*."

"*Never*. It was a *yellow* Seville. Yellow."

"Seville? You ain't had a Seville in years—way back there. Remember?"

"What?"

"Hell yes—that was back before the T-Bird. And them two Volvos. And that Porsche--"

"The *what?*"

"Now the *Porsche* was yellow. The Seville was tan—I think it was anyway. Yeah. Tan. But the Mercedes is blue."

"Mercedes?"

"Yeah. I finally sold mine y'know—did I tell you that? Last week. I got a Jap car now. You ever drive one of them things?"

"No—no, I always buy American cars."

"Since when?"

"Then you're saying I have a Mercedes?"

"Yeah. A *blue* Mercedes."

"Blue?"

"Yeah."

And it was like that more and more, the things I thought I had or knew not solid now but changing or gone moving like the roll of waves upon a beach. I went to see my doctor right after Peter Caldwell, Jr. mumbled into defeat—I think it was the next day in the afternoon, carrying a vision with me of the dipless tables at young Caldwell's wake as I waited for my name to crackle through the speakers hidden somewhere back behind the potted plants I'm sure I had never seen before—the hanging ones and others huge with shiny leaves and flowers in among them here and there, ancient-looking in their places out along the walls and inside boxes made of weathered brick. The nurses had been strangers to me, not a one familiar from my physical a year or so ago, and Doctor Ross himself, my oldest best friend Andy now was bald and wearing tiny glasses perched upon a nose he must have broken since our poker game a month before. It all had taken up three hours by the time we finally sat and talked inside an office newly furnished, one wall book-lined floor to ceiling and the others mostly glass that when I turned to look had brought to view a sudden and startling sweep of formal gardens and an orange grove and palm trees swaying in the breeze and something like a Grecian temple on a grassy knoll out toward the place I'd thought my latest car was parked. A red New Yorker, custom-built as near as I could tell and no Mercedes in it tip to tail.

"What *is* all that out there, Andy?"

"Huh? Oh. Well I'll say one thing about you, Rob—for free too—you *are* consistent."

"Beg pardon?"

"You always ask the same thing. Every time."

"What thing?"

"Look, Rob—how long have we known each other?"

"I'm not sure—fifteen, twenty years?"

"Try thirty, but that's not—"

"Thirty?"

"—the main point. No. The main point is this chronic hypochondria of yours. We've talked around it for years. I'd hoped that semi-retirement would help. Then the retirement. That it would give you opportunity to enjoy life a little more. Free you up to devote some quality time to your hobbies—the model boats and trains—"

"What? I don't have any model—"

"But it hasn't helped—not at all—no. Look, Rob, no sense in pulling any punches here—it's gotten worse if *anything*. No real improvement—"

"Why do you keep calling me, *Rob*? My name is Robert dammit—*Robert*—"

"—worse and worse. It's almost become a ritual. You imagine some ailment or other—perhaps from some television show or movie and—"

"Imagine? Imagine? What do you—"

"—come to see me for tests and we test you inch by inch. And find nothing. Nothing unusual. Nothing shows up.

And then we come in here to talk about it—about nothing—
and you stare at Memorial Park out there and ask me—"

"Nothing? There's *nothing* wrong with me? Are you
saying that I'm—I'm *imagining* all this—this *difference*—
the—the changes—the—did I tell you about the dip? Did I
tell you about *that* ? And my bedroom and the cars and all
the—"

"I'd think stress, you know. Before your retirement es-
pecially. I'd probably do that—go with that—for the record.
Prescribe another series of placebos and send you home.
But I can't anymore, Rob. I don't do that anymore."

"You don't?"

"No. Not anymore. Not since my recent—uh—
experience."

"Experience? Do you mean the hair-loss? The glasses? Your—your nose?"

"What did you say?"

"Then there's nothing wrong with me?"

"Nothing. No physical problems at all. Not even the
usual ones for a man of your age. And I will not be a party
to a lie, Rob. Not even for Evelyn. Not even for that dear
woman."

"Evelyn? *My* Evelyn? What does *she*—"

"It's over now anyway. All over and done with. We've
talked. I've even told my wife. I'd hoped you and Evelyn
had talked, but I see you haven't—oh God—forgive me,
Rob. I—I hope you can find it in your heart to forgive us

both. It was never anything but physical—believe me. No
real depth. We never really communicated—not spiritual-
ly—purely. We seldom even talked at all. And when we did
it was usually about you and Mona. But I've finally gotten
my own house in order praise God and I suggest you do
the same. I know I know—I know how you feel about
churches and religion, Rob, but you've got to forgive—
that—that's the key you see—for your *own* peace of mind if
for nothing else—forgive forgive forgive. HE could return
any day now. Any minute. Gives you pause, doesn't it? I
can see that it does. Yes. And you've come to the doctor
for help. Like always. In your pain and confusion you've
come to the doctor. Just like Evelyn. And all the others. But
what you need I can't prescribe, Rob. I can't write it down
and give it to you. No. I can't do that. But there *is* a place
you *can* go for help. For real and abiding help, Rob. Even
for an old agnostic like you—there *is* a place—even for
atheists—for flesh-sucking pagans—a place of purity—oh
yes there is! A place. To get your own experience. Yes!
What are you doing Sunday afternoon?"

"You and *Evelyn*? Are you telling me that you and Evelyn have been—"

"It's over. Long over. *All* over and done with. Mona was
very understanding. *She* received her experience last Sunday. It was *very* beautiful. So don't *you* dwell on the nega-
tive and maybe miss *your* chance—no, Rob—don't do
that—don't fall into that tired old trap—living in the past—
wallowing in old hurts and disloyalties—old dreams and
hopes—nosir—*you* look to today, right *now* –go, Rob—go
and be healed—"

I can't remember if I hit his nose square on or only grazed it on the second try, but he *did* bleed a good deal and called for altogether different nurses from the ones who led me in and weighed me and pricked my skin—he called in younger, tougher nurses with their hair close-cropped and sticking out in spikes beneath their caps and every one a shove and scramble with me to the door. And outside. Into what now seems a blinding light that somehow came on brighter than the sun. And hotter too and with a whirl of color in it like a port wine cheese-dip looking near enough to touch but somehow always just beyond my fingertips, a dancing there that took me far away from home. For days away I've since been told, police and Evelyn and Charlie Rourke's face too, their words a drone and filler to the blank spots everywhere—but cheese-dip pictures floating in and out, of what I must have seen before I made it here, clear-headed now and deep inside my shed, down in a cooling shade back with my gin and moving shadows near a slash of sunlight underneath the door.

But only cheese-dip led me on at first, back then (however long ago it was), the pictures I can see within it whirling as I must have walked and walked, the car (whatever it had turned into) left far behind at Andy's Park and Healing Show, back with an Evelyn I could almost hear in moaning joy down underneath a bald and crook-nosed best and oldest friend of mine, but far away and less and less and soon lost altogether to the things I saw and things I heard and nothing staying whole and nothing solid to the touch until I smelled (at first just faintly like a whisper-breeze upon my cheeks) a rich and heavy scent like pepper-onion dip or maybe bean-and-bacon swirl, a smoky thing that led me to a resting place at last. A resting place. The people black-faced there and laughing and a smoke about us all that curled its rich and bean-and-bacon-pepper-onion way and slow so slow across the light.

"What you want my man?" But nothing would come out, no word no matter how I tried. The dip and smoke and rich rich smell had pressed inside and thickened up my tongue, had pushed down deep around it and come back and trailing close and snug a sausage casing out behind.

"Whoa—get back now—he look crazy, man—don't he? Lookit his eyes—"

"Nah—hongry—he jus' hongry. Ain't that right, my man?" And black-faced men and women too and sitting down to eat, down with them there to push my sausage-tongue into a bowl of creamy dip like Evelyn used to make, down quick and catching all I could and back inside to chew and chew and chew.

"Good God a-mighty—hey now! Hey Stop 'im—hey? Get his tongue there—get it—"

"Put a stick in there—somethin'—he's 'leptic—it's a 'leptic fit—like Buster get—hold 'im!"

The rest is blurry gone and lost, but Charlie Rourke's voice somewhere in it near my bed, a rasp that seemed to float upon the antiseptic smell and half-light in a room I'd never seen before.

"My God, Bobby—God—I heard you scared shit out a them niggers. What th'hell was you drinkin', hey?"

Then finally home—the bedroom painted now, a light blue cover for the walls, no paper anywhere, and Evelyn gray-haired, wrinkled skin and hands like claws that shake each time she reaches for a glass. The pool out back is covered up, filled in, I guess and plastic-topped, the yard grown up in weeds and Charlie Rourke is dead they say and Andy- Best-Friend too and Mona now Chief Priestess of the Cosmic Savior Temple one block down and right where Evelyn's precinct club-house used to be. And me inside my shed each afternoon, with gin and dip I make myself and curly chips all thick and wide, the shadows moving near the door and forming shapes and one by one of my own things, of everything just like it ought to be.

The Klansman in the Closet

On the last day of his life, Clayton Burke is stuck between two moments in time— between two failures— between a little Jew's conversation with a nigger shoeshine and Billy Tucker's one shot at Jack Kennedy's passing head. Both are safely back in the same month and year—October 1960. He knows this (when he really thinks about it) but he also knows they won't stay back there and keep quiet. They have come instead to the *here*—with him *here* on the last day—to mix and mingle with his breathing in and breathing out and all the sights that jump up in his head.

Clayton sits down slowly in the grass, rests the shotgun in his lap, and leans back against the biggest oak in the Ponsell Woods. It is October again and a thin layer of cool wavers in the breeze that comes up somehow from the little lake on down past the pine and scrub oak and palmetto thickets out in front. The breeze ruffles his hair. It is a North Florida moment, mid-autumn, a good feel of shotgun stock and steel, and the twentieth century nearly done.

***

The Jew comes first. He doesn't smile, standing behind his counter in his little shop on the far side of the bowling alley. You can sometimes hear the rolling thunder back behind as he works on a boot. He doesn't notice Clayton standing just inside the door. In the shadows near a giant fern. The door is open and traffic sounds mix with the muffled thunder roll and crash of pins and make the words sometimes hard to hear. The Jew's right arm is scarred, a white jagged smear down in the thin hair just below his rolled-up sleeve. The nigger 'shine speaks first, blubber lips a suck and smack, and his words come solemn and slow. "What'd you see?"

The Jew frowns and bites at his lower lip. He lets the boot go as he answers. And the conversation runs on to the end. Clayton stands there waiting.

"A dead pig—bloated—flies—alive—moving. All that."

"Jus' that?"

"No. I saw more."

"What? C'mon—I know they's more'n that. What you see?"

"Lips. A man's lips."

"Lips?"

"Yes. And the sunlight."

"Sunlight?"

"Yes. It was cold."

***

The conversation stops there on one side of the oak. On the side the shotgun barrels point at. Out front are the pine and scrub oak and palmetto and the little lake down out of sight. The conversation stops there. Just for a little while. Just before the Jew tells about his family, about their dying in a pit deep off and lost out in another October morning. The nigger 'shine keeps shaking his wooly head. But, right now, Clayton doesn't remember many details past the sunlight and the cold. Just a few things there in among his failure to do what he had come to do. Just a few words and pictures in his head that hobbled along together with his failure to do Right.

***

The shotgun is an antique. German made. A side-by-side with ornately etched steel and a stock scroll-carved and polished rich and bright like the seat of a well-used rocking chair. It was Clayton's grandfather's favorite, and Grandpap had used it back in the 20s in Mississippi. It has four notches in the stock, near a rolling place that looks like a holly leaf. The old man had got him four with that one gun alone.

***

On another October day a week later and over in Jacksonville, Billy Tucker has a .38-55 Winchester Model '94 with a scope resting on his lap as he waits with Clayton to shoot Jack Kennedy as he goes riding by. Billy sits with his legs dangling over the side of a deer stand, hidden deep in the pine and palmetto, binoculars at the ready and a clear view of the airport road. Kennedy is due by in a few minutes. The newspaper has the route different. But Billy believes the radio.

"I'll get that nigger lovin' sum-bitch—one shot—"

"God, Billy—I don't know about—"Clayton speaks softly, sounding nothing like his *here*-voice.

"One shot—that's all I need. Please Jesus just give me one shot. Daddy says that bastid'll have niggers tellin' us when to take a piss—an' Jews too—hell, th'damn Jew's're behind all this anyways—y'know? Right?"

"I heard that."

And he had heard that all his life. Grandpap had joined the Klan when he was fifteen, back in 1925, and Daddy had done the same when he come back from Korea, cussing Truman and the niggers worse even than Grandpap ever did. And Clayton had wanted the same.

***

The gun glints in a flash of sunlight coming down in speckled dots full through the thick leaves and the moss. It feels warmer and then colder down in his place. It is always cold back in the failures. The first ones in a special way— the little Jew and Jack Kennedy.

***

He has come to scare the Jew. He has heard Mama and her friends talking how that one Jew is always smart-mouthing. How he's always looking at the young girls. How he'll cheat you blind if you don't watch him close. How he never shows no respect. Grandpap and Daddy say he needs a lesson in manners sure as hell. Clayton hopes he'll be the first one in. That he'll show them all how right he can be—how brave and straight. For the Race. To claim his portion. But it doesn't go that way at all. The Jew just keeps talking to the nigger 'shine and there is blood all out upon a fresh-fall of snow in some damn place far away and gone. Nobody even notices Clayton is there at all.

"They moaned—afterwards—"

"Your family? They wasn't dead?"

"Not all. There were many there. Others. They went before us. Hundreds. Thousands. Who knows?"

"How did you—"

"Not die?"

"Yessir—how?"

"I don't know. Luck. The pit was half-full—I—I don't know how they missed me—"

"You was in the pit your own self?"

"Yes—sucked down in it—I—I got away at night."

"Where did you go then?"

But Clayton doesn't remember any more. Just the feel of his belly turning cold and a taste of vomit fresh in his mouth as he suddenly knows he can't do it. Can't face a Jew and a nigger all alone. Can't make the words come out like Daddy and Grandpap make them do. Easy and straight and hard like a white man should. So he runs away.

***

The shotgun feels good, smooth and strong to the touch. He shuts his eyes and tries to blot out all the other failures—the years and years of never quite getting nothing right—never getting it over on nobody clean and straight. He had tried. He had done that all right. Tried. With J.B. Stoner once or twice and with the Flagler County Coonhunters. He'd almost seen one nigger burned alive— near Ponte Verda Beach one night in the mid- sixties. They burned him in the dunes but dumped the leavings deep in Sutter's Swamp, down past the Live Oak Ferry—Clayton only on the very edges of it all—that night making believe that he was hurt, that his leg had got caught in the barbed wire that Billy Tucker's uncle Buster liked to use for rope. It was always like that. Beatings. Two house burnings. A few shootings. Cuttings. He never got it right, never made it all the way in like Billy Tucker did. And then things changed. They all stopped fighting like they used to. Stopped caring enough to do much of nothing. Everybody watching then. Just watching. FBI and nigger-lovers like that goddamned LBJ. People starting to let the niggers win without no kind of fight at all. Just letting LBJ and the goddamned Jews lead the whole damn parade. Billy hated Johnson worse'n Kennedy but never got no chance for a shot. He wanted to though. He really wanted that. Right before he went to Vietnam.

Clayton squeezes his eyes shut tighter and lets the words come in from somewhere in between the Jew and the deer stand, maybe from out where the hawks nest deep in the Ponsell Woods. Billy's words seem to float right beside him in the cooling air.

"That sum-bitch is killin' th'white race, Clayton—killing it. Lettin' niggers in ever damn place—

"All I need is one time—one damn time—I'll blow his go'damned head off—I'll do it—"

But Billy got his own head blown off in the summer of 1968. In some place over there. Clayton still can't remember the name. It was nearly a year after Clayton himself didn't go, a heart murmur saving him from the nigger sergeants and the yellow-coons that Billy wrote about, his letters full of the Right-and-Straight all the way to the day he died. Billy's Daddy and the boys gave him a Klan burial, but Clayton pretended to be sick and stayed at home.

***

The scenes feel closer. The deer stand is stronger now than early on—Billy clearly there, slipping bullets in the side of the Winchester and smiling toward the distant road. "Kennedy's comin'," he says. "I can feel it, Clayton. Right down in my gut—he's comin' real soon."

And he smiles bigger and Clayton sees himself now watching the road through his own binoculars; through the pine and palmetto, past the clumps of people out along the road, the cars going by faster and a siren suddenly rising up, a quiver-wail and moan off toward Imeson Airport. Billy keeps smiling and aims the Winchester and adjusts its scope. It's all clear as day.

Clayton opens his eyes and sees a rabbit down near the line of palmetto at the edge of the woods. The scene stops, Billy still frozen with his eye to the scope; clear even in the pale sunlight, it stops while the rabbit sniffs the air. Its ears are almost translucent. And then it is gone, slipped back into the fronds, slowly at first and then a push off its hind paws and nothing left to mark where it had been. Clayton's mouth is dry and Kennedy's head is there in the binoculars, a side view and then full front toward the stand, his smile too big for his face. Just a second there and Billy's finger must have been squeezing on the trigger all the time it took to notice it and then, why exactly he never could tell himself in a satisfactory way, not ever, not once coming close over the thirty years and more since it had happened, why he slipped or fell into Billy's arm and made the bullet hit a tree by the sound of it, and by the time he can think clear again, Billy is trying hard for a second shot. But all that's left is a carload of girls with a big Florida flag flapping out behind them as they sit and wave from the back of a red convertible. Billy is furious.

"Go'damn go'damn—dammit all—"

"I—I don't know—I—I slipped or—"

"Jesus H.—Clayton—Jesus it's gone now for sure—"

And it was. Gone. The chance. Billy never got another one. Not nothing as clear and sure. He did try one more time (he said he did anyway) in Waycross, but it was too crowded there and no way into the buildings. And Dallas took away all the chances and then Billy got sent to die in Vietnam, the whole time saying he'd get LBJ for sure when he got home again.

"He's worse'n Kennedy—damn traitor—a go'damned white-nigger— thas all he is, Clayton—for sure—"

And after Billy died, Clayton got married and had kids. But then they all left him. Finally. None of them strong enough to stay long in the fight. Not one with even a spark of lasting righteousness nowhere down in their whole lives, not even a spark for all he did to bring them to the light. Gone now into darkness sure and lost. The wife first, five years ago, and the kids one by one and not a single thing left now at home except old clothes and memories about what could have been—should have been. And niggers and the other trash most everywhere you looked. Just like nobody had never done nothing to keep it all from going straight to Hell.

***

A dove calls from somewhere down in the swampy land to his right. Past the leavings of the deer stand and Billy and the rest. The Jew is back too far to see. The dove gives a lonely sound like it sometimes felt back when Grandpap told him of the bright and shiny way. The boys all riding in a dust storm come up from the horses' hooves, the Cross up front and bobbing high above the white robes going by. Fire come up quick to blaze the Cross all hot and crackling in the black of night and some to whoop like Rebel soldiers come back from the grave. And not one nigger face out on the street and not one nigger anywhere the horses thundered by and not one nigger but would moan and beg if he got caught someplace he never should have been. The boys gone riding down the righteous road toward glory in the night.

"They done what's needed doin', son. They done it free an' fair—"

And Clayton closes his eyes to let in Grandpap and then Daddy too, their faces strong and down close in among the way it used to be, their voices saying always how it needed to be done again. The robes out flying in the deep of night and hooves in thunder wrapped and Cross gone flame to open up the sky—ghosts of the Confederate dead all around in a horse-borne night. But now, all dreams and nothing more as he pressed down on the steel and wood there in his lap and thought about the niggers and the rest most everywhere you went. The world now owned by filth that fed upon the dream. Grandpap's voice comes in just at the end, a wheezing there and crackling sound like some old radio too plugged in to ever die.

"I fought over there, boy. In France. In Germany. I fought. And we was wrong, son. We was wrong all the way."

Out in the dark a flash of light and something like a white-robed horse all fierce and pawing at the ground and then sunk back in shadow gone away.

***

Clayton opens up his eyes. The rabbit is back. Just for a few seconds and then gone, a quick hop into the tall grass out front. Clayton kneels and settles the shotgun butt in the sand and gets the barrels fixed just so underneath his chin. He cut the gun down yesterday so the triggers would be easy to reach, so it would all go right. He wrote the note when he finished, and left it there this morning when he came down to the woods. Tacked to his first Klan robe. The small one he had outgrown by the time that Billy died. It is all together now. All the clothes. All the lost chances. And the note is with them. He remembers the words as he brushes over the notches on the stock and then pulls the triggers in a single squeeze to let the fire and light come down and all around and take him full away: *one less traitor to the race.*

In Defense of the Bruised Soul of the West, I Rise

He liked twilight. The sky often turned a decadent shade of lavender for a few minutes before dissolving into a color not quite blood but something very much like it. He enjoyed drinking gin and watching the sun set and letting the memories come and go like the birds that persisted in nesting in the red-tips beside the cabin's front door. Little birds. Loud and busy. And the memories usually were like that as well—short-lived mostly and yet full of a kind of life that jerked along in a tempo too erratic to measure with any hope of accuracy. It was New Year's Eve, 1999, and out toward the west, across the swamp grass and prairie came a sunset like none other he had ever seen.

He was sixty years old. His birthday had been two days ago and a local radio personality had brought him to the station for an interview, supposedly to ask him questions about his days of fear and trembling in the hard summers of a long-ago Deep South. The summers were famous—had been famous at least—but it was obvious by the third question that the young personality somehow had South Africa in mind instead of Birmingham and Selma and St. Augustine. They hadn't really meshed at all.

"Did you ever meet Nelson Mandela?"

"No. But I saw him several times on television."

It went on like that for a while and then some music and commercial messages came along to ease him off and on back home again.

He had been living in the piney woods of North Florida for about five years now. Since his early retirement from a graduate research professorship at Florida Landgrant University and his divorce from his fourth wife. He had over the years invested wisely and had married civilized women and had managed to have no children, and consequently was able to live comfortably and think and write books (mostly about those Deep South days) that the critics liked and libraries bought. These days he especially liked gin and sunsets, and he sometimes made the flicker of a memory come in close and stay awhile beyond its time. And when one did, he would seek a purpose there or reason that could make it something more than chance: This time it was the face of an old black man in Slackbridge, Georgia.

The sun was nearly gone, the sky filled with giant smears of near-blood and a purple-tinged copper color that seemed to bunch up and tremble down above the trees. It was mostly quiet out beyond the brief order of the front yard, out on the prairie, and only the little birds' rustling chirps in the red-tips near at hand served as counterpoint to the strengthening dance of that one memory. It had been forty years ago. Before his days of fear down in the marches and the hatred all around, back when he still was safely white. 1959 and in the center of the hottest summertime in years. He was home from school. It was just before his junior year at Auburn University, and he was working as a shoe salesman at Atkins Brothers Department Store in downtown Slackbridge. The store was not there anymore. And the little park was gone as well. But the black man's face was strong and so was all the rest, coming now quickly as if rising on the colors of the sky.

He sipped at his gin and watched the memory form in full. First, the heat. It had been noontime, and he was on lunch hour and had walked into the park seeking a shady place to eat his sandwich and crackers and drink his Kool Orange. He had bought the drink from a machine in the Dixie Den Newsstand near the Roosevelt Hotel. Neither Den nor Hotel survived past the 1970s, victims of urban renewal, torn down and their places covered by an interchange of two federal highways and a municipal parking deck. But back in 1959, all was as it had been for nearly a century (he was told this by his grandfather) and was nearly melting beneath a cloudless sky.

He was dressed in a white, short-sleeved shirt and tan slacks, Weejuns, and one of the shiny clip-on ties his mother had bought at a discount from some peddler who had gone door-to-door the previous spring. The heat made his shirt stick to his back like he had gotten wet and put it on without drying off even a little bit. The park was full of Coloreds, maids and a few old men, but mostly women were there, changing buses in the busiest part of the day, errand running, shopping, but mostly waiting on the right bus to stop. He passed by a few of them and one, a big deeply black man in patched overalls and a dented felt hat, smiled and nodded (taking off the hat in a quick up-and-down motion that revealed a shiny bald head and a thick purplish scar above one ear) and seemed, once all that was done, about to say a word or two but thought better of it and sat down instead up near the band-shell in a little wash of shade. The Kool Orange was sweating hard, the can all slick-feeling by the time he found a bench under one of the biggest oaks in the park. The bench was a splintered thing with a UDC brass plate pressed deep into one side of its scarred back and a nearby WHITE ONLY stencil nearly faded away. He sat down, not far from the black man, put his lunch and drink beside him and wiped at his face with one hand and pulled out his shirt and flapped it a bit with the other and tried to pretend it was cooler in the shade.

Lunch went quickly. The sandwich was peanut butter and the crackers were limp and only the drink, still nearly cool, felt good going down. He had just glanced at his watch and noticed that he had nearly twenty minutes left when he saw the white men enter the park on the side opposite where he was sitting, out past the band-shell and down toward the river, maybe forty or fifty of them all carrying walking sticks or canes of some sort (he thought at first), but as they came closer he could see that they were axe handles, some with nails driven through them and a few with what looked to be barbed wire lashed atop them in a way that made him think of a rooster's comb all flared out. The men seemed to be marching together, two rows at first and then three and then in pairs or threes as they came into the park all along the river side, up (he guessed) from the streets that stretched right down to the dark water of the St. Gadarene's River, up from the little stores (the Cracker shops, his mother called them), the places that sold such things as axe handles and barbed wire and nails and maybe even let you put all three together right there free of charge. It didn't seem real at first. None of it did. Sitting there on his lunch break and watching the big black man stretch out for a nap and over beyond his resting place fifty or more men beginning to beat down on every Colored that they saw and could get close enough to hit. It seemed like a television show. Even the sound was like that. Like his family's television set—the old one they had back then—muffled and surging up and falling back—but in the park, at least, one sound had stayed strong and mostly clear— a wailing scream that woke the black man up.

***

The gin was nearly gone. The sunlight was all but over too—a few red spaces left between the clouds and trees now gone to dark. An owl hooted somewhere and a cricket chirred close at hand. The evening would be a long one, he knew. Long and full of the memory that now would keep itself alive, that would roll along on its own internal motion, on full toward whatever stopping place it might decide was right. To show him clear a vision of what used to pass for his own life, a moment when the old way caught in shame had shivered in the light. He finished off the gin and let the night come on.

***

The park had turned into an almost visible ache and moan of pain, alive with beaten Coloreds everywhere, and those not yet brought down were running through the thickness of the heat, falling over each other and trying to get onto buses that now refused to stop, heads and backs bleeding and arms and legs all covered up in blood. He had knocked over the remains of his drink as he stood up and almost got hit by a passing Colored woman, heavy in the white uniform of some lunchroom or hotel, her back all wet with blood and a man there bringing down with all his might a blow that left her twitching near a row of boxwood and a clump of orange marigolds. The man was red-faced and shone with sweat, a glistening that looked like oil spread evenly all down his thick arms and out across his neck and face with care. He had licked his lips and kicked the woman once or twice and glanced over toward the bench and smiled and nodded and then run off to find somebody else.

The big black man had first crouched up close to the band-shell, had tried to make himself almost meld with its dark painted wood, to blend into the deep shade around its base, but the other men were everywhere and no place clearly was secure. So he came straight for the bench, straight as a purposed shot and got behind it like he some-how was an essential part of an Auburn student's summer day. He stood there shaking, hat long lost, and bald head shining as a red-haired white man came up pushing out ahead of him hard with the butt end of his axe handle a slender colored girl, her arms scraped and bruised and a deep cut across her forehead that made her face seem stuck in an expression of open-eyed surprise. Her dress was in tatters, and as the man butted harder, she fell over on the grass near the place the black man stood, her hands grasping his ankles, fingers tightening even as the white man kicked her in the side.

"Hey now—hey there, bitch—c'mon now—leggo that boy—" The white man's voice was soft, a contrast to his kicks and to the moaning sobs of the girl. "Hey now—here Cap'n—he'p me—" He said the words almost casually, aim-ing them at the bench as if help was a certainty, a sure thing given all the conditions of the day. "Hey—this here your boy, Cap'n? This here uncle yours?" He had nodded at the black man.

Now it had all seemed real, up close and certain of contour and substance, a true moment in all its fleshly parts. The black man looked first at the girl, down on her bloody back and surely full into her eyes as she raised her head up toward him through her pain, and then over at the bench, at the young man already edging toward the safety of the bushes out behind. The black man's eyes were wide, grown wider with each moan and cry for help the girl let go, a near-burning in them at first that seemed to make the rest of his face disappear—but quickly, with each step the young man took to safety, the eyes began to cool, the face came back in terror first and then in something else, a something not so much of living flesh and bone as of a shadow not quite formed and well beyond ability of words to hold.

"C'mon here, bitch—you—leggo the boy by God— go'damn you, boy—go'damn you—you step on back out a here—step on back now—"

And the black man was hit several times and began to buck and jump, boots pounding out a clogging step-dance in the grass, the girl's grip breaking then, the white man pulling her on up and free. The black man stumbled backwards a few feet and began to run, an awkward and bloody stomp and shuffle and jump over shrubs and through a trashcan, jumping high at times like someone had set both his feet afire, and running harder straight on out the far end of the park and finally lost to sight. The white man shook his head and laughed.

"My God—you see that?" His voice was still soft and his laughter came out all mixed up with the moaning of the girl. "Hey Cap'n—he'p me get this here took care of—c'mon an' he'p—"

But he made it past the bushes instead, and back to work only fifteen minutes late.

***

The night was a deep one. He stood up and yawned and let the memory go away, whirled off into the mist of the prairie and the sounds of night birds on the wing. He had listened to the nighttime before. It never ended when you thought it should. Never.

A Covey of Georgia Klansmen with Flag and Two Dogs

It was the most klansmen Bobby Rockman had seen on the Long Bottom Road since the All-Georgia No-Mixing Rally back in 1955. It even seemed bigger than the 1945 Trans-South Reunion. Like both of those times, however, he sat on his front porch and watched it roll by—the pickups and cars pushing dust up and back along the road for miles and miles, covering his front yard with a pale white that looked like his wife's biscuit dough. It was five miles to the old Methodist campground from the front yard, and the traffic was getting thicker and louder by the minute.

Bobby was impressed this time and a little surprised too at the numbers and especially when he saw the High-Sheriff himself, Winslow "Trout" Scroggs, come by on a high-stepping gray mare that had one ear splayed toward her left eye like something had tried to cut it off but failed. Trout waved and sidestepped the horse onto Bobby's front lawn. Red robes were strung across the front of the saddle, giving it the look of a festive blanket pulled too far forward and bundled together like a rolled sleeping bag.

"That you, Bobby?" Trout's voice was loud but still barely audible above the truck and car boil and blow behind him on the narrow road. He was dressed in full county uniform, big Stetson hat and all, an oversized badge on the left pocket of his khaki shirt catching the sunlight and making it dance up on the highest leaves of the tall hedges thick-growing along the front porch.

"Yes sir, Sh'iff. Yes sir. What all's goin' on?" Bobby could hear Edna May back in the kitchen banging around some pot or other and singing with the radio. He couldn't quite make out the words, but the tune would come in and out among the other sounds from time to time and seemed somehow familiar.

"You ain't heard then?" Trout kept the horse sidestepping in front of the porch. Out on the road, an old school bus came cranking and clattering and then to a quick stop right in front of the gate to Edna May's vegetable garden. The windows in the bus were all open, and it was full of robed klansmen, unhooded, white sheets mostly but a few red ones like Trout's, and every one of the men singing along to some banjo and fiddle tune that had a shouted "nigger" in it seeming like every other word. And then the bus sputtered back to life and set off a roll of dust and a bang of black exhaust that made Trout's horse whinny and rear up. But Trout reined her in. "It's in all the newspapers. On TV too. You ain't heard?"

"No sir, I expect not. No Sir." The last thing Bobby remembered on the news was some cows being field-dressed over in Toombs County by what the newswoman said might be Satan worshippers. He and Edna May had worried about that for nearly a week. Until the beans began to come in.

"Whoa now—whoa!" Trout took off his Stetson and wiped his face with a shirt- sleeve. Setting the hat slowly back on his head, he pulled on the reins and made the horse come as close to a stop as she seemed able. Her eyes looked wild.

"What's goin' on now, Sh'iff?"

"Whoa now—go'dammit whoa! Whoa!" The horse snorted and seemed to be trying to stare down a portion of the tallest hedge, one eye fixed and steady on the upper-most leaves. "You like my horse, Bobby?" She seemed about to rear up again, but Trout changed her mind with a sharp pull to one side on the reins, making her kind of shuffle a little to the right, down dangerously close to Edna May's baby azaleas.

"Yes sir. She seems ok to me."

"Whoa now—whoa!" And he dismounted and tied her to a maple sapling near the front steps. More trucks were passing, and another and larger school bus, and then one oversized convertible with five red-robed and hooded klansmen, two of them waving the biggest rebel flag Bobby had ever seen. The Sheriff snapped to attention and saluted and then did a little jig-step that got everybody in the car making a sound mid-way between a yodel and a scream. "Whew now—them ol' boys're pure tee crazy, I'm telling you the truth there, Bobby. Crazy. Whew now."

"What's it all about Sh'iff?"

"How old are you, Bobby?" Trout patted at the horse's neck and smiled.

"Do what?"

"How old. How old are you?"

"Why you know I'm near ninety. Eighty-eight. In June."

"And Edna May?"

"Don't know for sure, but I figure at least eighty."

"Damn, Bobby—and you ain't never joined up?"

"Joined?"

"Us, Bobby—us." And he waved a hand out to include the still busy road.

"No sir. Never did. Never did." The radio got louder in the kitchen—more music coming clear, and a few words too.

Keep on the firing line…

And then *something/something* and a high lonesome fiddle coming in with an almost moaning squeal and slide.

"Well now, you ain't never been no trouble, Bobby. Even my granddaddy said that. No trouble at all."

"No sir."

"You just never joined—and they asked you plenty times, right?"

"Yes sir they did."

"And you just kept saying 'no'."

"Yes sir. I ain't much for joinin'."

The radio got louder, and the traffic out on the road began to die off a little, just a few dented pickups and one old black Cadillac and then nothing at all. The Sheriff reached for the reins, and then remounted and pulled the horse around to where she was nearly pointed to the place the cars and trucks had disappeared, a short rise of ground that curved left down toward the river and the old Methodist campground. They always met out there.

"Well you ain't never caused no trouble, Bobby. No sir."

"What's it all about this time, Sh'iff?"

"A nigger Miss Georgia, Bobby. They done elected a nigger Miss Georgia. Up in Atlanta. Yes'day."

"Do what?" The radio was louder yet and Edna May was trying to sing along.

> If you're in the battle for the Lord and right,
> Keep on the firing line...

"Georgia's sendin' a nigger to the Miss America!" The horse reared for a moment and began to pull hard toward the road. "A go'damned nigger. Jesus my lord, Bobby." The horse settled a bit and began pawing at the grass near Edna May's biggest azalea bed. "But we ain't going let this stand. Nosir. I'm just glad Daddy died before all this here."

"Yes sir, Sh'iff. Yes sir." The radio crackled some now, like static had settled in to stay.

If you'll win the victory, *brother,*
You must fight…

"It jus' can't stand, Bobby. It can't."

"What you boys plan on doin', Sh'iff?"

A last car came by, slowly, a big one with women in-side, three in back and two in the front, with a red-robed klansman at the wheel, hood pushed up on the dashboard and looking like some kind of sleeping puppy. The women appeared to be singing, but none of it would come clear of the radio and Edna May, steadily growing louder and louder behind him in the kitchen.

Keep on the firing line, oh line,
Keep on the firing line—
Time is running short,
Jesus comin' soon, brother…

"There they are, Bobby. Some of our best—an' one of them lucky gals going be Miss White Georgia. Yes sir. We going make our own." And he rode off into the dust, the horse prancing a little and making a snorting sound as two good-sized walker hounds clambered hard out of the piney woods across the road and fell in behind. Bobby shook his head and went inside. And then only the radio was left, come free of static and pushed out strong down toward the slowly settling dust:

Keep on the firing line….

Waiting for LBJ

Two boys in cowboy hats stood on the lower steps of the Supreme Court Building. Beyond the floodlit dome of the Capitol, a red light was visible through an occasional clearing in the swirl of loose snow. Above and behind them, the massive doors of the Court were partially obscured by shadows and the snow lay deep on the steps and the wind rustled the moon pie-sized "Lyndon B. Johnson For Vice-President" buttons pinned to their overcoats. Stamping their feet, the boys turned toward the big doors and moved up a few steps, slowly, deliberately clearing space on the stone. Snow, caught in a gust of wind, now whirled around their feet and seemed to be moving upward, sheet-like, into the shadows behind them. Their pants flattened against their legs and their hats bobbed and the ribbons on their buttons fluttered.

"There it is, Ricky," pulling his hat down more firmly on his head and wiping at his nose with a gloved hand. "You still think LBJ can stop 'em?"

"If anybody can. Kennedy won't even try. That's why we done all this anyways. Worked our asses off for Johnson. Right? LBJ's our last hope, Daddy says." Ricky took off his glove and scratched his chin; a roll of pinkish fat showed briefly beneath his scarf in the dim light. He pulled the glove back on and flexed his fingers. "Kennedy loves niggers." Below them on the sidewalk, a stooped man in a loose-fitting overcoat seemed to materialize out of the swirling snow. Raising his head, he removed and replaced his tattered hat and waved toward the boys. A car horn sounded twice in the distance and someone rattled a cowbell near the Capitol.

"Ain't you boys out a little late?" The stooped man seemed to be smiling up at them.

"No sir. We're staying just over yonder," Ricky pointed toward the dark corner of the Court. "Just over there a ways."

"Cold night though, ain't it?" The man pushed his boots into the deeper snow on the bottom step.

"Yes sir."

"Hey, Ricky," speaking in a whisper, the other boy shook his head and stamped a few times on the snow.

"What?"

"That man's a nigger—see? Look. Ain't he?"

"You boys here for th'big show tomorrow?" The man now stood on the first landing, a few steps below the boys.

"Yes sir. We worked in the campaign."

"Ricky," the whisper was more insistent, "I said he's a nigger." The man had turned toward the Capitol. For a moment, there was only the rasp of his heavy breathing as he stared into the snow-blurred landscape of jumbled and indistinct trees and traffic signs and blinking lights. Then, from somewhere in the distance, another car horn sounded twice before continuing, stuck on an undulating single note.

"Yeah boy," the man shook his head slowly and glanced sideways up at the boys, "I seen a lot of shows in my time. I even recollect Mr. Hoover's. Yes sir, I do remember that one." He rubbed at his chin and made a clucking noise in his throat. A sudden whirl of loose snow made it appear that he was moving in and out of shadows, giving his head a bobbing motion as he stood there smiling and clucking. "How old are you boys?"

"Seventeen. We're both seventeen."

"Seventeen? Lord-a-mighty, you just babies. Just babies. You got any idea how old I am?"

"No sir."

"Ricky. Ricky, let's," the whisper was lost as the stuck horn stopped blowing and a trumpet suddenly sounded several discordant notes toward the Capitol. Laughter and shouting followed and the man moved sideways up several more steps, to a spot almost level with the boys, snow covering the tops of his boots.

"I'm seventy years old. Seventy. You boys is just babies. I was a porter on the old Silver Meteor when you boys was just love twinkles in your daddies' eyes. Where you all stayin' at?" Almost involuntarily the boys backed up a step, both nearly falling on a patch of ice, and the man's laughter seemed to punctuate, to fill in the blank spaces between notes from the trumpet and the resumed cowbell rattles and the shouts. "Go easy there, now. Don't fall. You get your pants wet if you fall. Where you staying?"

"Over there," Ricky pointed again and felt a cold lump in his throat, remembering his father's warning about the night people of Washington: war stories of brothels and payment for acts somehow too vague and illogical to ever be really true or even possible.

"But, Daddy, why would anybody pay you to do that?" His father had seemed to wince as his mother rattled some pans behind them in the kitchen.

"Never mind, just you watch out is all." He had looked for his father's eyes, but they had already returned to the sports page.

"Why would anybody want you to crap all over them?" The eyes had left a headline about the Packers and seemed to be on the verge of rolling.

"Look, I said to just be careful up there. I know what I'm talking about. You don't. And watch out for the niggers in particular. They're the worst there are. You understand me?"

Ricky couldn't quite make out the eyes of the old man below him in the snow, but he could clearly see his hands shake and hear the clucking which was chicken-like, yet cadenced in a way approaching a hum or a whistle.

"You southern boys, ain't you?"

"Yes sir. Georgia."

"Georgia, huh? Where abouts in Georgia?"

"Ailey."

"Ailey? God-a-mighty now! Ailey? My my my. I was borned near there. Vidalia."

"Ricky," the whisper was almost louder than normal speech, "Ricky, let's go on back to Mrs. Smith's."

"Ailey, huh? I been there. Ain't been back tho'. Not in near forty years. Who's high sheriff there now?"

"Mr. Brinson."

"Not Mr. Harley Brinson? No. No, it couldn't be him. The boy? Mr. Harley's son?"

"Yes sir. Mr. Artel Brinson."

"No. His name was Thacker. Red-headed boy?"

"I think he got killed in the war."

"Lots of boys lost. Lots of boys." He bowed his head and seemed to be studying the snow as the wind whipped it over his boots and settled it into the creases of his pants. "My brother got shot down in Vidalia." He looked up at the boys and nodded his head. "Forty years come this March." The trumpet held a high note as a chorus of whoops, fragile in the distance, seemed to be trying to form themselves into the words of a song. "An' you know what Mr. Harley told me?"

"No sir."

"He told me I'd best just forget about it and get on with bidness. Get on with bidness." He turned again toward the Capitol and began to move down, testing the snow with first one boot toe and then the other. "You boys get on home. It's too late to be out here." He stopped near the sidewalk and the shadows again gave him the appearance of bobbing movement as he stood in the deep snow. "New men coming in tomorrow." His voice was reedy, the clucks more wind-rasp than chicken-like as he adjusted his hat and pulled at the collar of his overcoat. "New day tomorrow. Getting on with bidness." And he was gone, into the whirling snow as if a curtain had been lowered quickly by a skillful stagehand, on cue, but somehow unexpected by the audience.

"Ricky, he was a nigger. Damn."

"I know that."

"A damned nigger an' you called him, 'sir.'"

As the boys reached the sidewalk, the snow swirled behind them softly over the steps and their footprints and Ricky's tears felt like tiny needles on his cheeks.

Right and Wrong

IT AIN'T RITE. The sign was nailed to what was left of a discarded billboard rising up sixty feet easily from a clump of palmetto on the edge of the piney woods off the shoulder of the highway. Rt. 62 North. Busiest highway in northeastern Florida. Near the town of Old St. Marys. The lettering on the sign was black on a dingy white background. Lubber Janks had made the sign, and had put it up a couple of weeks ago. Lubber liked to climb up to a narrow ledge he had nailed in place near its bottom and wave to the traffic. Sometimes he did this twice a day. Sometimes he did it three times. And once or twice he had missed a few days when he wasn't feeling so good. Lubber was fifty-six years old and every so often would work at a sawmill and sometimes for the Town of St. Marys hauling garbage. No wife. No kids. No kin at all (not counting his daddy's two older children who ran off while Lubber was not even a year old)—nobody there since his daddy died over twenty years ago. And nothing left of Daddy but five acres of junkyard and a mostly made-up house. Today Lubber was ready to begin his true work. Finally ready. After thinking it all over. Finally ready.

He had pushed two scopes into his coat pocket, strapped a knapsack full of ammo tight on his back, slung two rifles over his shoulder and climbed up to the ledge an hour ago. Right before dawn. The traffic was already humming along down below. *Tourists,* he thought. *Heading for Disney World,* he thought. "Heading for Hell," he said out loud. It was two days before Christmas.

He was taking his time getting settled in. Thinking back on that fat county man in his too small uniform, huffing and puffing up to the house a month or so ago. He sprayed when he talked.

"Mister Janks—you can't keep all this here," pointing to the junked cars and bikes and all the rest that took up nearly five acres of what used to be piney woods and scrub oak thickets. JANKS JUNK had been his father's business and Lubber had kept it going for the past twenty years— after the old man died mid-sentence on Christmas Day. He had said: "I think I'm going to get me a…" and then he slowly fell over into his toast and eggs. Thinking back on it, Lubber sometimes felt that Daddy was just about to say something about the junk needing more room (there was no question about that), that it needed someplace to keep on growing (all that was easy to see), but the fat county man just kept on talking about pushing everything back and out of sight. "Now you got to get you a fence up, Mr. Janks. To hide all this here mess you got. You can see it from the Interstate and the law says you got to hide it. Or cart it all away. Your call."

Lubber remembered licking his lips and then saying: "An' what if I don't?"

And fatso come back with: "We'll cart it away and bulldoze all the rest, Mr. Janks, and send you the bill. You got a month. You hear me, now?"

"Yeah," Lubber had said, and the sign had gone up about two weeks later.

Lubber snapped the scopes into place once he got settled in up on the ledge, and then he took his time with the first shot—sweeping right and left—settling finally on a little red sports-car with a froggy-looking man inside. It was a clean shot. Froggy swerved into a van and both hit some kind of tiny clown-car and the whole mess rolled off the highway and into some trees. The smoke was deep black. The junkyard had come out to play.

And Lubber did it ten more times—hitting at least ten more— with black smoke now on both sides of the highway down toward the county line—a quarter of a mile away but in the scope near enough to touch and smell—ten more times and then another ten going back and forth between the rifles before the first siren sounded, a high whine from the direction of Old St. Marys. He reloaded both rifles and licked his lips and swung out and picked off a Greyhound Bus. This time there was fire on the county line, streaking up inside the blackest boil of smoke he had ever seen. There was a slight breeze now, blowing from the east, from back toward town, cool and touched it seemed ever so soft-ly by ice. Like it was up on the mountain years ago when his daddy had farmed and trapped and hunted and fished. Before they made everybody come down here to this place. Before the junk yard and way before county fatso come into it. Lubber had liked all that—the mountain and his Daddy (Mama no memory at all and the two older kids long gone before Daddy moved on down to here)—it was good. Right. It all smelled fresh. Felt right. A live feeling like what the scope brought in just before he squeezed off another round and then another and the highway all boil and shooting red and the sirens now close by and flashing blue-lights every-where it seemed both right and left and the ammo getting low. He let two cars go by—old jalopies—and then a truck with a busted front grill came through the smoke and he let it clunk on by—and then he nailed a bright green SUV that seemed to buck up and down a few times before veering off the road and into the median and smack into a row of state-issue dump trucks. The driver of the SUV had been some kind of woman, he thought—long blond hair and a moon-face all puffed out and fish-belly white.

A bullet hit the sign—and then two more and he quickly dropped to his knees—losing one of the rifles—watching it fall and then bounce on the ground down below before seeming to break up into pieces. Black smoke was drifting closer and closer and the sirens were all around him now, like hornets come out quick from a rough-used nest. And then, he was somehow back on the mountain, before all the bulldozers and the new houses begun to pop up everywhere and before his daddy said it just wasn't no damn use to none of it no more. And Mama was alive and them older kids maybe still there and never once a siren nor a county fatso making sure nobody ever saw what wasn't clean and new and strong. Especially them out there on the highway. Especially on their way to Disney World. To that Rat Kingdom. To where the Big Rat lived. He'd seen the double-wide signs with the Rat smiling and wav-ing. Seen the ads on the TV too. Everything pointing on down south. Fun and sun and dancing with the Rat. And everything and everybody clean and new and sparkly. But, his Daddy had liked the junk. And stayed put right here. And Lubber did too. The only true and abiding work there was once the mountain was gone. Until today and this here. Daddy had even wrote it all down one day—burned it into these two thick wooden slabs he had. And then nailed them to the junk yard gate: IT AIN'T RITE. EVERBODY NEEDS A HOME. AND EVERTHING. IT JUST AIN'T RITE TO DO IT NO OTHER WAY. And Lubber stood up and smiled real big in the memory—police clumped down below and memory now all smoke and fire-choked, black-crinkling all along its edges from the highway heat, nearly gone away, and then a cracking noise and weakening of the knees and finally everything gone fluttering still and finally falling quick into the end of everything at once.

Down among the Whispering Pines

Professor Stuart Watson was lost for a while. Five hours. Word went out. Campus Police into it the second hour. And then the Chief of Plants and Grounds and Housekeeping, Mose Rivera, found him down by the discarded and headless statue of Monidieux O'Malley, down in the deep piney woods near the dried-up duck pond, O'Malley's headless bronze torso and outstretched arms green and slick with guano and a misting rain. Professor Watson was asleep (Mose said later) between the outsized feet of the founder of Pee Dee River Technical University, no longer lost but certainly confused of face and dressed in his graduation finery (minus mortar board), his doctoral robe torn in at least three places. He was smiling when he woke up, Mose said, smiling and humming a tune almost familiar.

"Mose!"

"Dr. Watson—why? Why you say all that stuff? Why you get gone like that? Everybody been lookin'—why you out here?"

"Out where, Mose?"

"Here—out back here in the woods—why?"

"Who knows, Mose? Who knows?"

And then he had stood up and saluted the remains of Founder Monidieux (victim of a vaguely religious attack some ten years before by a visiting professor from India who also smashed fourteen stained-glass window depictions in the University Chapel of seminal moments in the life of Charles Darwin). Mose said that Professor Watson then stretched and finally walked slowly in the general direction of the now empty football stadium, trees soon blocking a clear view of his progress, and Mose and Monidieux both left solidly and silently behind.

He walked. Toward the football stadium. Trees thinning out ahead and the campus suddenly there. No more misting rain and everything at first clean-lined and almost painfully green. Graduation was long past. And five hours beyond gone as well. Lost. Memories? Professor Watson tried, but only President Broome's frowning face and flashes of light and finally Mose-in-the-woods would show themselves. Within his eyes and out around as well: flashes of light real enough to walk within, it seemed, memories strong enough almost to hold his weight. Professor Broome was first—the strongest and the longest one of all.

"Listen here, Watson—I don't care for language like that. You understand me? I won't allow it. Nosir, I won't."

"Language?"

"You know what I mean."

And the Chief Administrator of Pee Dee River Technical University (master of all he surveyed from his privately endowed office building) turned a faint purplish color as he began a steady pounding of his fist on the empty surface of his glossy, oversized desk—the office itself deep within the Executive Suite and served (it seemed almost continuously) by two eager and shapely administrative assistants. The scene was earlier today. Graduation day. Before the five hours came and took it all away (except for those flashes of light and then the sturdy Mose, of course). President Broome kept pounding and frowning and spitting out words from his light-purplish face.

"Who do you think you are anyway, Watson? Who?"

"Y'know, sir, I was just thinking about that very question this morning at breakfast—and I finally decided that I really would never know how exactly to..."

"Stop it! No more, Watson! No more! Not one more word or so help me God I'll fire you on the spot! Pulitzer Prize or no Pulitzer Prize. Understand? How much you think we're going to stand for just because you won that damned thing ten years ago? How much?"

"Sir—I—"

"No more now! You got me?"

"Yes sir."

"Good. I mean, you're already on probation as it is. My God. And then this whore-mongering business, I..."

"Whore-mongering, sir?"

"Yes yes—your tirade at the Executive Council meeting yesterday—"

"No sir, not me."

"What?"

"I never said, 'whore-mongering'."

"But I have it that..."

"I did call them all whores, sir. I did that—but nothing further. What they actively practice with their status (and perhaps malady) is strictly up to them. In fact, I said as much right after..."

"What?"

Then came the lost time. Not quite all at once. Graduation first. But all around it near or far thoughts of his thirty years in service ripping and tearing one by one, one after another, from a time when he was young and still believed the possibility of truth, a stout and steady soldier in the fight. But darkness mostly. Fog-like. Rolling and boiling and roiling along and over him as he must have surely left the Chief Administrative Officer all purplish, sputtering like he had done a month before when Professor Watson had pointed out the Obvious (from the presidential podium no less) and before all the gathered employees—a huge virtual orange banner with black lettering stretched in light behind him and proclaiming (in a pulsing almost-dance): TECHNOLOGY CELEBRATION: PEE DEE RIVER TECH #1. The meeting had been called to acknowledge the two thousandth on-line course—installed and going live just that morning in the Division of Comprehensive Logistical Humanities—a course in "Cognitive Everythingism" being taught by the Divisional Dean himself, D. Demetrius Barth, a mighty man of letters and with standards high and strict.

Professor Watson had even said something to that effect from the audience right after Barth began to speak, finally securing the podium itself—pushing Barth aside to everyone's astonishment—stating the Obvious quickly and (he had hoped at the time) clearly enough for even the yawn of nodding heads on the very last row to take inside and keep. The Obvious. It got him put on probation. Today? Who knows, Mose? Who knows? But the podium voice was strong and clear:

"I'm certain all will agree that since there is no way to tell the cheaters from the true-hearts in on-line courses—and since we all likewise know that our University will never give up the on-line easy money—I think it best to delete all mention of plagiarism and cheating in general from the Student Code of Conduct—in strict fairness to all and in the best tradition of a University that never met an intellectual sin it did not savor first and then turn full into a profit sound and sure."

Professor Watson passed the football stadium and headed downhill toward where he thought his office ought to be. The fog was mostly gone, but his sight was blurry, eyes a bit sensitive to the late afternoon sun. His robe felt all wrong, so he discarded what was left of it in a brightly painted (school colors—orange and black) dumpster and began a half-jog down the winding path that came out past the Life Sciences and Bio-Managerial labs and within a few hundred feet (he hoped) of his office. But nothing really seemed the same, not holding firm in either memory or to sight—different—at first slowly and only out along the very edges, and then swelling inward toward him wave-like and deep in places—dark-caught and trembling out before. Different. He didn't remember the woods, in particular, that somehow he was jogging through—a few strange buildings on either side and a smell of worms out all around. Underbrush. No people. Hot. Humid. So he shed his shirt and kept on jogging.

And a few flashes from the lost time rose up to hover on ahead and then fall down and full away the closer in he came.

-----The First: Two pleasant-looking people, a man and a
       woman, over-dressed in a casual way and with a cap-
       and-gowned too-skinny girl in tow, standing right in
       the path and listening to a blurry facsimile of Profes-
       sor Watson:

       "Yes—yes, I did say that," his voice is close-on-the-
       same, but not quite—sounding like it's coming up
       from a very deep and static-filled well. "Your daughter
       is a butcher of the English language—an apprentice-
       moron—and a confirmed—even dedicated plagiarist.
       Yes. Not that such a thing matters anymore. But—I
       thought you would want to know anyway—
       considering all the money I am sure you have spent
       and plan on spending on her. Yes. Or perhaps you
       would want to know just for the sake of knowing. Or—
       to produce a memory for the family scrapbook. Yes."
       And then bending in closer and nearly whispering:
       "Word has it she's well-connected. Yes. Well-
       connected." Winking here to fill in the necessary nar-
       rative gap.

And then the flash was gone, burned away like a photograph in a fire, black blisters puffing up and then all smoothly gone to ash. He was again alone on the path. Hot. Humid. So he shed his pants and shoes and socks. It was growing hotter on the way and the buildings were gone in a whirl and pumping push of the fog come back and deep and all around. The flashes continued—one after another—one and then another and then—

-----President Broome again—properly purplish in a deeper more steady way—consoling the pleasantly over-dressed couple and their well-connected cheat of a graduate.

-----Campus Police in a quick gust of clear, talking into their shoulders.

-----A bit of sky showing bright and then the faces of several colleagues too cowardly even to speak of the cheats and whores all around all around alive, alive-oh.

-----The National Anthem—sound and sense joined, solid and somehow marching in its own words and making every note count.

-----A stage with colleagues' faces everywhere—some smiling, most not—sounds of cursing—deep-throated-Professor-Watson-voice roaring up above them all and "Whores! All Whores!" floating at first and then dropping fast upon every face there was.

He was nude now, all clothes gone, left behind, and the pathway choked with brambles and sounds like baying dogs from somewhere back behind. He jogged on and then stopped. Listening to a wind come up above him in the pines, a whispering moan that seemed to say that all was lost and gone down in the whoreson dance that played out fierce both back behind and up ahead and over and around him as he stared full-faced into the falling fires of what was left of what he started out to be.

Professor Stuart Watson was lost for a while. Five hours. Word went out.

The Secret Life of D. Demetrius Barth

No one was supposed to know. No one. Ever. D. Demetrius Barth had been so careful for so long now that he
himself had difficulty believing in even the possibility of it
all. Nothing physical remained—not even a photograph or
videotape. He had seen to some of that after the fact, and
even during the dangerous time itself had been careful to
stay free of the press and, as best he could, to distance
himself from the others (the once-upon-a-time friends) who
had raised him up in the Cause and stepped out with him at
the proper times. Years. Decades had passed since he had
left his home state of North Carolina for the west and an
expensive education and a successful career. And he had
felt safe for a long, long time now. Ph.D. in Cognitive Logistical Analysis (UCLA), Master's degree in On-line Education
(Stanford), a Bachelor's in Comparative Literature and Logistical Analysis (Arizona State). Cushions and barriers.
Years of teaching (University of Illinois/Washington State)
and publications (three books and forty-five major articles).
Cushions and barriers. An African-American wife and four
delightfully-shaded (now grown-up) children. Cushions and
barriers and barriers and cushions. And then—for reasons
not entirely clear to him at all, nor to his wife—a return—
near retirement age—to a Southland he barely recog-

nized—to Pee Dee River Technical University in Harvey County, North Carolina—with nothing like it used to be out all around him day by day.

He had been hired as Dean of the Comprehensive Logistical Humanities Division, more as a place to mark the time until he could drop gratefully into the arms of the State and ample personal savings to live out his remaining days in peace. To mingle with the grandkids and maybe take up fishing or simply sit and smile at all the life gone passing by. But something had gone wrong after a few years (with less than one to go until retirement)—had indeed been wrong right from the first (he knew this whenever he found himself in its presence)—had been there right from the moment he shook President Josiah Broome's massive hand and noticed that only the two of them were White. Two blonds shaking hands in stark contrast to the others standing near. The two Personal Administrative Assistants. The University's chief attorney. African-Americans all. And—he now knew—right from the very beginning, Blacks seemed to be everywhere a dominant theme most every place he went. On campus. In town. In his deeply-shaded neighborhood. Casually so. Whites there too and Asians and Hispanics and some he couldn't tell exactly what they were— but, moving, mixing all together calm and quiet. And—it bothered him. Deeply so. And opened up what had been safely tucked away (he thought) since last he wore a hood and rode fierce down within a deepening night.

That last time was some forty-five years before. A sweltering, drought-caught summertime in Green County. He was not far past his teens and robed and hooded and riding in the middle car with Rufus Shields and Red Hence and one other tall boy in back with the tied-up and mouth-taped Negro—an uppity albino boy that somebody said needed a lesson in manners. The other two cars—front and back behind—were full of once-upon-a-time friends all around, and everybody heading for the county line—to Cherry County and the logging trails hard by Wilson's Swamp. It had taken about an hour to get there and settled in—the boy moaning all the way and trying to break loose when Red pulled him out of the car and into the circle of headlights there in the taller grass just off the trail. Red yanked him back and full into the kicks and punches of the once-upon-a-times—everybody taking turns—D. Demetrius favoring the belly and the groin, not hard at first but steady-on and full-toed in a pattern up and down. And then it got out of hand. The boy got one arm free and clawed Red's face and Red pulled out a pistol and shot four times before anybody could even speak. And four more times he shot. And then he kicked and stomped the head so hard that nothing much was left.

Nobody said nothing. Robes got stained as they stuffed what was left of the boy into this old burlap sack that Rufus had and weighed it all down with chains and tire irons and some big rock D. Demetrius found in the tall grass nearby. And then they packed everything up and drove to the Yadkin River Bridge and dropped the whole mess (pistol and all) into the strongest part of the current rolling by. Nobody had said a word. Nothing. Only some whippoorwill sounding off from the higher ground across the bridge. D. Demetrius had burned his robes that night— the next day heading for the west after taking out of the bank the money Grandpap had left for his education as well as his own savings. No parents still alive. No brothers or sisters. Just the once-upon-a-times and a Cause too fear-some to maintain, all blood-drenched and moaning out around it in the night. He never went back and had never heard another thing from nobody there that night. He did find out years later that the once-upon-a-times were all dead or pressed down deep in nursing homes. That the boy was never found. And that no one seemed to know a thing about anything that had happened on that night. He was safe. Soon passing for a longtime soldier in the fight for equal rights—sound and true and freedom's man right down the line.

Until last week, nothing had surfaced of his discomfort—as if living elsewhere all those years had at least given him a strength to withstand the shock—had made it easier to take—or ignore—the mixing all around—the almost-dance of maybe not a blind acceptance, but at least of something well past the borderline of simple toleration—no shame now in touching, kissing, hugging, a casual closeness there that surely would have brought down violence quick and clean back in the days when he still rode. The South had changed. He thought that at first, of course. His South maybe. Perhaps not all, but here at least—together every day a kind of rolling proof that nothing had remained the same. He lived in that belief for a few years. Until last week when it all began to fall apart.

The first time it had been a white student, a freshman football player. D. Demetrius was watching a practice— near the sideline—and the young man was taping his ankle.

"Hot one today." D. Demetrius had been watching a particularly tall black student, a running-back of some sort, plow over three whites guarding the goal line.

"Yeah boy, it is." The young man had looked up and nodded his head.

"You like playing with spooks?" And the words had come from somewhere, gone past his teeth even (it seemed) before he noticed they were formed at all—defenses gone away. Barriers and cushions knocked aside almost as casually as the young black running-back continued to push himself into the end zone play after play. And then the young man spoke again.

"Not much. No sir. But they in the game." He had sighed and continued to tape his ankle.

"Bet that stink's hard to get off, hey?" And he had been horrified to hear another burst come forth—words there as if they were skipping his mind altogether and forming somewhere in his very blood and bones.

"Yes sir, it is. Daddy says he sometimes smells it on me when I come home. Makes me shower, y'know?" And he had smiled this time. A sweet smile, almost coy and pouting. His eyes were painfully blue. "But I'm on full scholarship, y'know? And they's niggers aplenty in the NFL. Yessir, they is." And he finally had finished taping and began to put his shoes back on.

"Well—don't let it rub off on you permanently, hey?" And D. Demetrius's feeling of panic and fear were nearly palpable as he listened to words that he had no apparent control over—no forethought of—nothing there strong enough to stop them pushing out beyond the safety of the shell he now knew wasn't nearly strong enough to keep inside the man he always was. No real change had occurred, he realized, watching the young white trot out onto the field and quickly knock down the running-back on the next goal-line stand. But there was joy in that. D. Demetrius felt it deeply. Joy in watching the black get up, take off his helmet, and shake his wooly head. Joy.

And then it happened more and more. In the campus bookstore—to an amazed white cashier who later said she wasn't quite sure what she heard, but the tone had been "hateful":

"And how far did you chase the nigger for that blouse, honey?"

Once on the elevator in the Life Sciences Building, to a plump black secretary carrying her lunch back to her office:

"Lordy Lordy Lordy—how you does love them fried chickens, mmmm mmmm."

To an astonished Nigerian colleague between classes in the hallway of the Internet Lounge, after sniffing loud and long and smiling a few times as he nodded his head:

"Well, at least you ain't a Mississippi nigger—whew boy! Know what I mean?"

And on and on until it seemed he couldn't stop the words from coming out at all—no control—no way to keep them down inside and sleeping like he thought they'd always stay. Again and again and again—little slip-ups in class—bigger ones in Department meetings—all finally leading to the biggest one of all. He had carried a watermelon into the Convocation— today—into the very face of the entire University—faculty, staff, administration—students— all gathered together to formally welcome in the coming year. Until then, only a few had heard. So far only a casual number had been touched. The very few along his way. The most important, his wife. After many little episodes, the biggest one yesterday at breakfast:

"Do you really like our jig president? Really?" He had paused while eating a poached egg on toast, fork raised and a smile on his face. "Do you? Imagine—a coon in the White House. My my my."

"What?" His wife had dropped her coffee cup and seemed just before sucking in her tongue.

"Jig President Obama—y'know—that coon you voted for."

"D—what's wrong with you? Are you trying to make a joke? Is that..."

"No—no joke. Well. Yes, joke. Big joke on us all. Big joke. Big damned joke. Never should have let 'em up, y'know? And that means especially you and your kind. Yes sir."

And he had nearly snarled out the final words. His wife had left quickly. Packed and left for New Orleans, he somehow thought—although she was from Seattle . New Orleans it had to be, though. Down with her own kind.

And then the Convocation and the end of the line. A watermelon—a big, long, and thick watermelon carried like a baby up to the podium for his part in the festivities—the unveiling of all the newest on-line culture courses—those new humanities offerings that kept on growing, fatter and fatter as if fed on some sort of virtual fertilizer, time-released and guaranteed to make things better woman to man and all points in between. He raised up the watermelon and said simply:

"Behold, niggers, your God!" And then he fainted dead away.

***

The hospital room's walls were deep-lined with something like puffy burlap. An off-white nearly. Not quite gray but definitely mixed. D. Demetrius Barth was thinking, slowly but steadily, as the doctor came through the door, a syringe poised and a definite smile on his too-white face. D. Demetrius thought he knew the doctor right away. His head fixed now and body healed and clothes no longer soaked in blood—and raised up wholly just a little bleached and mottled from the river water down below.

The Orphan's Lament

It should have been done right and not so messed up.
There should have been a lot of stuff said—a whole lot of
stuff. A lot. Nothing like what really happened. He knew that
much. Clearly knew that he had been robbed. Not given his
due. Not taken seriously by anybody. Not even by Daddy
himself (in spite of what he did and said right there at the
very end). Not by the nurses surely. He expected that. They
barely even noticed he was there at all. And the doctors—
the doctor, that is—only one and he was so fat he wheezed
every time he raised his head up from reading over the
thick chart. He was pink too. Very pink. And bald. He never
spent no real time there anyways. Right at the end, he
popped in some tiny earphones, and Jonas never heard
nothing but some mumbles coming out of him about
"cheeseburgers" and "fries" and "nurse—see to it!" as he
pushed through the room and made it into the hall.

Jonas's father died at 9:25 A.M., July 12, 2002, in St.
Lucy's Memorial Alzheimer's Ward. The rest of the family
had long been gone when it happened—after squeezing
the old man's hand or kissing him on the top of his head.
Jonas had hung back against the wall—the last to arrive
and fresh from a patch of jail time (again) for drunk-and-

disorderly and resisting arrest. The family seemed to sniff at him as they passed by. Like he was some kind of fruit that had gone too ripe or had dog crap on his shoes or something. And then, except for the nurses, he was finally alone with the old man. He came in close and then that one word come out—strong and clear all right but nothing much to hold to beyond the thing itself: "Outstanding!"

Jonas had noticed that the old man's eyes were bright-looking and that he was pretty much smiling when he said it, looking right at Jonas and even reaching out to take and squeeze his right hand. And then he shut his eyes and breathed out a long sigh and left it all behind. And that was it. The nurses fussing over the various dials and knobs and the rest. Nobody noticed Jonas leave. Later, at Wild's Corner, he sat mostly alone at the bar and tried to make sense of it all to Buddy, the owner/bartender/bouncer.

"'Outstanding', huh? You sure that was it?" Buddy wiped up a pool of something like beer from a place near the big peanut bowl. He tossed the stained rag down beneath the bar. "'Outstanding'?"

Wild's Corner was pretty small, only a few tables and half-booths and the big curved bar, and it was late afternoon, a shaft of light flooding inside each time the padded front door opened up. It was Jonas's favorite. Since forever.

"Yeah. 'Outstanding.'" He sipped his beer and noticed Alvis Binns come in the door, two other millhands with him, and all three arguing about something not clear to nobody but them. "And none of them damn nurses seemed to care when he went. I done told you about the doctor and the rest. Family worse of all. Couldn't wait to get shut of it."

"You did say that doctor was pink?" Buddy poured three big ones for Alvis and the boys and slipped them down the bar. Alvis always sat near the restrooms. At a booth that jutted into the room at an odd angle. The place was filling up. Two strangers now sat on either side of Jonas. Shots and beers. Buddy quick about it all like always. The juke-box crackled alive. Hank Williams again. Buddy liked Hank Williams. Big picture of him over to the right of the cash register. Jonas liked to stare at it sometimes. The eyes looked friendly.

"Yeah. Pink. Damnest thing I ever saw too. Fat. Short. Pink. And no time to waste on Daddy, boys—I tell you the flat truth there—no damn time to waste. Nosir. I think he had to go eat or something."

"'Outstanding', huh?" Buddy looked up at the ceiling, a slow sweep up past the heads at the bar, up into the smoke slowly rising and dancing a bit each time the doors opened and the sunlight came in. It was darker outside, though. Nighttime coming on. Buddy shook his head and cleared his throat. "Not much to go on there at all, y'know?"

"Tell me about it. And he was smiling when he said it."

"Smiling?"

"Yeah. A big-ass grin even."

"What'd *you* say?"

"Say?"

"Yeah—when that 'outstanding' come out—what'd you say?"

"Hell I didn't say nothing."

"Nothing?"

"Nothing." And it did seem strange now that he hadn't even said a word in return. But them damn nurses began to fuss around and Jonas was still mad about ol' Pinky and the family too. Nobody seemed to care he was there at all. And him just out of jail. "I just watched him fold. Right down he went too. You could feel it."

"What you mean, feel?" Buddy waved at Big Chick, the foreman at the lumber yard, coming in hard with a woman who looked like she'd been shredded and put back together in the dark. Big Chick always sat near the jukebox, but there was a couple of Mexican-looking guys already there.

"Yeah. In the room. It felt light."

"The room, you say. The room felt light?"

"Yeah. It wasn't nothing like it was before."

"After he said 'outstanding'—after that?"

"Right. It felt lighter."

And right then the shredded woman began ragging on the two Mexican-looking guys and Buddy grabbed his axe handle and stepped over to where Big Chick had begun to stamp his feet and put down a fierce line of cussing that came out all full of spit and coughing. It all got real quiet then. Jukebox clattering into silence just as the Mexicans left real quick through the front door. The quiet stayed awhile too. Buddy didn't like no upsets while he worked.

Jonas sipped at his beer and watched Buddy put the axe handle back somewhere down under the bar.

"Lighter, you said. Right?"

"Yeah."

"Well I don't know about that. Lighter?"

"He was smiling and said 'outstanding' and it got lighter. That's the way it went."

"Just like that, huh?"

"Yeah. And nobody seemed to care one way or the other. Just like when Mama died."

"She say anything?"

"I don't know. I was in jail."

"Oh."

"But nobody acted like nothing special had happened when I got out. Six months that time. Trespassing and public urination and resisting."

"Too bad you were in. Maybe she said something and maybe he was adding on to it. Y'know? That'd sure clear it up."

"No. I don't think it was nothing like that."

"Why?"

"Mama never much talked anyways. No. It wasn't nothing like that." The bar was too hot now, air-conditioning not doing much to clear away the smoke and smells and the rest. Jonas got up to go. He laid a ten down on the bar—the money returned to him just this morning by an undersized guard over at the city jail.

"Keep it, Jonas. On the house. It ain't every day you lose your Dad." Buddy pushed the crumpled bill back toward Jonas's hand.

"I know. Yes sir, that's so. Not every day." And he stuffed the bill into his shirt pocket and headed for the door. Big Chick was bouncing the shredded woman on his knee and Hank Williams was suddenly on the jukebox, guitars whining and the man himself pushing hard into "Cold, Cold Heart."

It was still light outside, nearly dark but only fully so deep under the tall oaks out front and along the sides of the bar's parking lot. Crickets chirred and a dog was barking off in the distance. Car horns sounded and a siren came up close by, out on Phoenix Avenue. It smelled like supper everywhere. Like everybody was firing up their stoves all at the same time. Like chicken was frying everywhere and biscuits was baking. It smelled good. The beers were working on him, his head light and a warm feeling in his belly, and he needed to take a piss. No time to go back inside. He spotted a big tree off to the side, toward the start of the houses that stretched down Fifteenth Street all the way to the little park by the grammar school. He held onto the tree's ridged side and let go, thinking about how much easier it had been when Mama died.

An Ancient Enemy

Fishbait kept the snakes safe behind his shack in a partially shaded and divided pit that he had dug himself. There were rattlers on the right and cottonmouths on the left and for the past four years he no longer had to crate and haul them the sixty miles round trip to Ponta Gorda and the Institute. Nearly every week in the late summertime a bright black-and-orange striped van would pull in from the highway and negotiate the few hundred feet to the pit, and after a time of noisy struggle a college boy would step free of the boxes and the poles and give him money for the snakes and then drive north as casually as if the load were oranges. It had been an especially good season, late July and early August having netted Fishbait almost $1000.00, and on this particular Friday he sat rocking on his front porch watching the sun try to cut through the shimmering haze which had settled over his one-acre plot like wood smoke over a roof on the near side of a mid-winter freeze.

Even the occasional sea-breeze felt hot, and beyond the dunes across the highway he could just make out a few gulls sailing slowly toward McCoy's Point. Several dark clouds had begun to gather to the northeast. From the porch they seemed no larger than a man's hand, but

James L. Fortuna, Jr.

Fishbait knew that a storm was coming, had known it since sundown yesterday when the sky over Sutter's Swamp looked as if it were burning yellow and then red by turns, great shafts of light seeming to have burst from the clouds or risen up from the cypress like solid columns, tilted and angled and holding up something ponderous but unseen. It had looked like that the evening before Hurricane Eleanor knocked flat downtown Seacrest City and gouged out the boardwalk and left not even a footpath where the Ocean Highway had been. Rubbing his chin, he wished the van would hurry so he could send out the snakes and secure his pay with the rest of it in the dented tackle box out back under the seat of his only good boat. The clouds were growing larger.

He tilted the chair back and raised his boots up on the railing and thought back to the last snake he had caught, nearly a week ago, a seven-foot rattler he had almost missed by staying too long with that new Presbyterian preacher. The snakes were thinning out, losing ground to the condos and resorts and moving further and further into the brush and swamp. Out front, the haze was stirring, the breeze feeling good against his face and chest and coming from the direction of the clouds. He scratched the back of his neck and listened to the tree frogs clacking above like toy motorcycles on a wooden floor. It had been a while since he noticed any traffic on the highway, a few dune buggies and the wrong van and a school bus with FIRST PRES. CHURCH painted down the side. He remembered thinking that the new preacher was strange, fat and dressed in army clothes and wearing a hat like the mailmen use. They had talked a long time but the man never seemed to listen, making Fishbait wonder if he maybe had a midget radio or something plugged in his ear to catch the baseball scores. But he at least was different from the last preacher who posted his land and never went outdoors except to get in the car.

The right van passed by almost before he noticed it, leaving Fishbait with his one good hand raised just a few inches off the armrest.

"Damn fools." He slid his boots off the banister and bent forward and frowned out toward where the van had disappeared. He knew it could not come back for at least half an hour—until it reached the first turn-off in Stone Crab Beach.

"Must be new boys this time." The clouds had spread themselves out along the horizon, giving the dunes an appearance of being topped in black. The air had cooled and the breeze seemed to have been soaked in salt, at times making his eyes water and his bad arm throb. It had been two months without a proper wetting and he hadn't had to use the pit cover once.

"Might as well set. Let them new boys get th'joy ride out of their systems." The FIRST PRES. bus came back, children's faces at all the windows and a faint sound of singing reaching the front porch of the shack. He wondered if the new preacher was on the bus, fat face and funny hat and all, singing along with the children and maybe eating what was left of the bag lunch. Then he remembered he had seen him earlier as he sped by in his new car pretending to be watching the road until it was almost too late to wave back. But Fishbait had kept waving and smiling his best smile and watching the car until it was gone.

"Damn fool college kids. An' a storm comin'."

The clouds had now begun to build upward as well as out and the breeze was strengthening and his bad arm throbbed and made him wish one more time that he hadn't gone shrimping that day with Ansel Carter and got himself hung in the net and pulled sideways into the boat's propeller. That was the day he got his name and lost interest in the sea. And after his arm got mostly fixed, he had turned to snakes almost by accident, noticing an advertisement stuck on the cash register one morning at the Seahorse Café as he sat there sipping at his third cup of coffee and trying to get Bob Davis to put some Elvis in the jukebox. It had been a yellow flier from the Ponta Gorda Institute with big black print that asked for reptiles and promised top dollar. At first he had chased away more snakes than he caught but soon, gradually and steadily, he felt that he had come upon a way of life that suited him better than anything else he had ever tried to do. And working the land wasn't near as lonely as the sea. At least he had the snakes and trips to Ponta Gorda and visits by the college boys who sometimes let him tell what he thought about or saw while seeking out their cargo. And that was why he went to see the preacher, just to talk about the woods and what he did and how he sometimes felt the hand of God Himself there resting on his shoulders when he pushed down on the head of some big snake and took away its fight. But that preacher hadn't seemed to hear, had even backed up when Fishbait came in close to make sure he was talking loud enough. He wished the college boys would hurry. Across the road he could see two surf-fishermen top the dunes and shuffle down and out of sight. The whole northeastern sky had gone blue-black.

Fishbait stood up and leaned against the railing. Lightning flashes could now be seen in the approaching clouds and the cool breeze was stiffening by the minute. He glanced out at the highway and sighed. Maybe the college boys had stopped for supper or found them a girl. He had known a woman long ago, with hair so red he sometimes thought that each strand had been taken out and painted one by one. He could no longer remember her name or how her voice had sounded but that hair had never gone away, as clear in memory as the preacher's face all fat and eyes that squinted at the setting sun and jaw so tight it seemed the bones were coming through the droopy flesh. The woman had worked at the old Café and left it during a bad drought, gone back to her people in Arkansas or Tennessee and never told him why. He guessed he had loved her and her hair the most of all but years gone by had dulled all feelings past his hunger and an almost rage that pressed to come back strong when something like a preacher or a dream showed up to touch him unawares. The red-headed woman vanished in a jagged burst of light out on the sea. He thought he could hear the waves as the van slowly nosed its way onto his land.

"About damned time." And he stepped out in the yard and waved them on in.

The van had backed up near the edge of the pit by the time Fishbait reached the pathway behind the house. There was sand in the wind, stinging the back of his neck and reminding him of the bites of yellow flies out on the swamp. One of the boys was standing at the pit, long poles resting near his feet while the other one unloaded the special boxes from the back of the van. Fishbait glanced over his shoulder at the wall of clouds all black and crackle-flashing, come closer now and moving fast like dust and dirt before an angry housewife's broom. He wanted to talk to the boys, new ones this time, and not cargo-talk neither or pay but all about the preacher and the woman and the other things that he had kept apart from talking but which now were rising up in him like a wind come off the sea.

"You Johnson?" The boy at the pit glanced at Fishbait and then turned toward the van. "Move it, Paul. Damn storm's almost here."

"You boys get lost?" Fishbait peered over into the pit and smiled down at the movement, thick and dark and coiling in the dying sunlight. They always knew when a storm was coming.

"What?" The boy looked startled, stepping back a few inches from the pit and watching his friend carefully stack the boxes.

"Get lost? Saw you go by."

"Yeah, well—we never saw your road." He craned his neck to look over the rim of the pit and whistled. "Damn. How many you got down there, Pops?"

The other boy spread out the boxes and wiped his forehead.

"Ten each—rattler and moccasin. One of them rattlers is near seven foot." Fishbait noticed the other boy's smile, a hard one like the sailors showed in Seacrest City, thin-lipped like a dog all set to snarl. "Maybe over seven foot."

"Bull. Mark—let's get 'em."

Fishbait stepped aside and watched the emptying, the coiling black and white and then the flashes of dull gold come up to twist awhile and buzz and slap into a box. It was going too fast, the boys' hair ruffling in the wind and sweat come through to stain their shirts and nothing more than cursing and a buzz and slap and buzz and slap again to mark the time gone by. The other boys were slower, had stopped to listen and tell jokes from box to box and maybe take a sip of corn when they were done. But these two jerked and raced like lizards up and down a wall and didn't seem to even notice he was there at all. So Fishbait stepped aside to watch and think and let the cooling wind push strong against his back. The big rattler was giving them trouble; twisting loose just shy of the box, he broke their hold and flipped himself backwards into the pit.

"Shit! Get 'im!"

He remembered the day when the big rattler had waited for him just minutes and feet from where the preacher stood, near the place where the grass from his land ended and the pine and scrub oak and palmetto thickets got their start. It had been moving slowly toward the denser brush, moving through the sand like a moccasin in swamp water, head raised and tongue flicked out just when the loop dropped down and Fishbait felt a jolt come in by his good arm that traveled to his toes. The hiss and rattle sounded like a truck tire going flat.

"Jesus, Mark—get 'im!"

"Won't hold—oh shit!" Watching the dark tail slide over the rim, massive rattles whirring like locust wings and dropping out of sight, Fishbait smiled and licked his lips. He had played that snake for what seemed like an hour, falling down at least twice and finally getting it into the special sack the Institute had given him and tying off the opening down on his knees in the hot sand, his bad arm throbbing from the effort and the last rays of the sun washing over the scrub and palmetto and turning everything into the color of pale gold. He had sung to the snake as they moved toward home and the pit, walking through a twilight alive with the last sounds of day birds and the dry clack and buzz of unseen insects and the deep croak and stutter-squeak of frogs already greeting the coming darkness. He had felt good with the snake hanging down from the pole behind him all safe and noisy in the sack and the song had made the darkness go away.

> *You ain't nothin' but a hound dog*
> *--cryin' all the time,*
> *You ain't never caught a rabbit*
> *--an' you ain't no friend of mine.*

And that was the last snake he had seen out there. After nearly a week of poking through the scrub from Stone Crab Beach to the San Marco Lighthouse, he had given up and waited on the van.

The storm had reached the dunes across the road, hanging there as if trying to decide where to go, sending out stinging rain-drops mixed with sand to pelt the van and men.

"Let's go. Just pay the old bastard." One of the boys was already loading up the boxes. His back to the wind, Fishbait stepped to the pit. The sun still shone through the cypress further out in the swamp while on either side dark clouds crept closer, seeming to reach out for what was left of the day. Thunder drowned out the thud of the closing van doors and one of the boys was hurriedly writing on a pad, the tips of multicolored sheets of paper flapping up and down like flags on a circus tent.

"Here. Sign this." He held the pad with both hands, thumbs pressing down on the paper. The other boy was starting the engine.

"Ain't got no pen." Fishbait slowly turned around, wind making his eyes water.

"Shit—here take this," one of the sheets almost tore away as he fished in his back pocket for a pen.

"Where you want me to sign?"

"There—in the middle. See that X?"

"Yeah. Nine rattlers? You only payin' for nine." The pen felt greasy in Fishbait's fingers as he passed it back to the boy. Above the wind and sporadic rumble of the thunder he thought he could hear the hiss and whirring of many snakes, as if the pit were still full and the boys had just arrived. The boy almost lost a blue sheet of paper when he ripped it off the pad. "You only payin' for nine?"

"Yeah nine. Can't get that big one. No more time, Pops. Here's your money—receipt—it's all there. See you next trip."

Stuffing the paper in his pocket, Fishbait turned back to the pit. The sounds of the van were soon lost, thunder and the hissing below him gradually coming together to blot out even the memory of a lost woman or a preacher's disapproving face or the hard smile of a college boy. The sun was down and lightning flashes showed him where the long board was lying and helped him see well enough to slip it down at an angle into the darkness of the pit.

Like Any Tourist

On Sunday afternoons during the season, Fishbait Johnson liked to hike down to Reptileland and mingle with the people there who came from as far away as Japan. He would dress in his best clothes and lock the front door of the shack and use the old Sutter Trail which bypassed the Ocean Highway to curl its way through the sawgrass and palmetto and pine thickets before ending abruptly at the fringes of the parking lot. There were always many cars on Sunday afternoons and people dressed in short pants or bathing suits and wearing strange-looking hats. He liked the Japs the best, with their big smiles and their cameras clicking like field locusts on an August morning. He sometimes pretended he was one of them, part of a group of tourists, an uncle or somebody's grandpa who they pretty much left alone until he had something to say. Most of the people were polite and the owners, Marc and Buck Potter, had gotten used to his once-a-week appearance outside the front gate. But until last Sunday, Fishbait had never gone inside, preferring instead to sit and watch it all from a bench near the fifty-foot gator statue that straddled the walkway and provided shade up to the entrance with its tail. There were royal palm trees there and he could nod and smile at the people as they passed him by. A big sign—with drawings of gators and snakes and lizards had been put up on the edge of the walkway: SUMMERFEST 1981.

Although it was late Sunday morning, Fishbait hadn't gotten out of bed; lying instead on his rumpled sheets, he stared up at the streaks of sunlight that came through holes and tears in the window-shade and cut across the walls and ceiling like bright but dusty bridges sometimes dancing in the breeze. Since before dawn, he had kept thinking about last Sunday and all the things he saw and heard when the Potters had let him in for free. The offer had surprised him, Marc Potter seeming to appear like magic just as a particularly long line of clicking Japs shuffled their way toward the gate. "Yeah I mean it. Can't see nothing out here." And he had followed Marc and the last of the Japs under the tail of the gator, past the aluminum turnstile, and into a place like nowhere he had ever been before.

"You might want to see the milking first thing. Over there," Marc had jerked a thumb toward a tall glass silo wedged in between two live-oaks. "The gator wrestling'll start in about an hour. Just look around. It's all on the house."

There had been a sizable crowd behind the brass railings that circled the silo, so Fishbait had decided to walk instead along a sawdust trail that seemed to dead-end at a row of connected boxes. It had been hot there, steam still rising from the last of the early morning dew, and all along the trail he kept bumping into Japs who bowed and showed their teeth. The boxes were cages, glass enclosures in which snakes and lizards slept or tried to hide from or ignore the line of spectators who passed slowly by to gasp or giggle or carefully click off frame after frame of film. But one large diamondback had made him pause, its tongue flickering into the glass like a candle flame caught in a draft. Fishbait glanced to one side in time to see a fair-sized Jap almost tangle his camera bag on one of the rough wooden plaques that stood near each box. The one in front of the rattler was hard to read. The big Jap turned to Fishbait and smiled.

"Pretty one. Yes. *Crotalus adamanteus.* They get verra big. You see yet the *ancistrodon piscivorus piscivorus*?"

The words had seemed to blur into each other and Fishbait stared hard at the man for a few seconds as if expecting to hear them repeated in English. But the camera had begun clicking almost before the man stopped talking and the rattler continued to flick out at the glass while behind it a mate's head pushed free from the end of a fern-covered log.

"I catch them things," Fishbait had said to no one in particular, "for th'Institute. The one down by Ponta Gorda." But even a red-headed man and his wife and skinny kids didn't seem to hear, preferring to pass quickly by the rattler's box and regroup at a taller one a few feet away. The big Jap was already there.

Fishbait could read most of the plaque this time but the coil of yellow, brown and black beyond the people worried him, its eyes red-looking even in the shade and the rest of it seeming strong enough to push on through the thick glass and swallow up one of the skinny kids without even slowing down. The Jap's voice was cheerful, mingling strangely with the camera clicks and the murmurs of the red-headed family.

"Ah good. Ver'pretty. *Reticuratus.*" He stopped clicking and turned to Fishbait. "I first read about in book. Ray-
a-mond Dit-a-mars. You know a him? He American."

The smile was broad and invited agreement, making
Fishbait think of a preacher right before he asked for extra
money. They all moved on, Fishbait pulled into the group
like he had been with them all his life. He barely saw the
other snakes and lizards and walked right past the Galapa-
gos turtles and only got a little bit behind one time before
finding himself on the bottom row of a small amphitheater
staring out at a paunchy Seminole powdering his hands
with what looked like rosin. There must have been two
hundred people jammed in together on the hard wooden
benches. Fishbait sat between the last of the skinny kids
and the Jap.

"He fight arrow-gator. *Arrow-gator Mississippienis.*"

Fishbait had tried to smile back but his lips were too
dry to do little else but twitch. The skinny kid next to him
was squirming, bumping her legs into his with each movement and jarring his bad arm. He winced and tried to shift
his hand closer to his chest.

"You inna war?" The smile was gone and the Jap
seemed to be just before asking if there was anything he
could do. Fishbait was getting used to his speech.

"No. Shrimping accident. Long time ago. I hunt
snakes now."

"For here?" His lips had pursed and his eyes widened, reminding Fishbait for a moment of the movie-Japs
he had seen, eyes almost round behind big glasses and

every other one with a buck-toothed grin you could open a bottle on. But this Jap's teeth were smooth and white and even and he wasn't wearing glasses at all.

"No. For th'Institute over at—"

"For here?" The eyes had remained wide, expectant, as if Fishbait hadn't said a word.

"No." He spoke so loudly that the skinny kid jumped once and stopped fidgeting.

"Ah. Verra pretty ones a here. Look good."

"I never sold none here."

And then he had watched Marc Potter walk out from behind a bamboo wall pushing what looked like an over-sized rubber bathtub on wheels. The Seminole had belched and slapped his hands together, white powder floating off into the still air in all directions. Marc stopped in the center of a hard-packed dirt circle and walked over to a micro-phone that jutted out from one side of the bamboo wall. He waved at Fishbait.

"You ain't seen nothing like it, ladies and gentlemen!" As Marc began to talk, Fishbait wondered why he had nev-er thought to ask the Potters if they needed any snakes. Reptileland had been open for five years, but he never once had bothered to mention how he made his money.

Marc was continuing his introduction: "And Chief Mikey Palatka will do it the best you've ever seen! Chief Mikey—c'mon over here and say a few words to the folks."

It sounded like a plague of tree frogs when the Seminole reached Marc's side, all the cameras seeming to go click at once and then again and again, peppered with flashes that made the sun light beating down on the amphitheater feel hotter than it already was. Fishbait had pulled out his bandana and wiped his face. He had only been there about an hour but somehow it seemed like days.

"Ladies and gentlemen, Reptileland takes great pride in presenting for your entertainment, Chief Mikey Palatka—great, great, great grandson of Osceola and southeastern champion gator wrestler!" The Chief picked at his nose and adjusted his beaded vest before taking the mic from Marc. Fishbait wondered where they got all their snakes. The Chief's words went by almost as fast as the Jap's.

"—yessir an' you know that's the truth now. But I'll beat 'im—he's tough and tricky and mean and fast but I'll take 'im first throw." The applause had startled Fishbait, bringing him back from a daydream in which he had managed to drive all the rattlers and moccasins out of the swamp and into one big glass-covered pit where he could sit all day and sell them by the foot and pound to the Potters. The big Jap nudged him in the side and smiled.

"I see this before. You ever?"

"No."

Two shorter Seminoles had helped the Chief raise the gator out of the tub and place it carefully, jaws tied shut, on a wooden platform. The clicks had stopped as it was untied and the Chief straddled its back slowly, fingers clamped tightly around the still closed snout. And then there had been a frenzy of movement, Fishbait watching through widening eyes as the gator flopped upward and then over onto its back, with the Chief pressing into its jaw and rubbing its white belly like he was polishing a platter. The gator had appeared to be sleeping as the Chief raised his hands in victory and stepped clear. Marc began the applause.

"There you go, ladies and gentlemen! That's why he's champ!" The Chief had walked once around the sleeping gator and then jumped back up on the platform. Everything went real quiet as he flipped it back on its belly and held tight to the snout and motioned to the two shorter Seminoles to run over and help tie it shut. Then they all three had jumped down and held up their arms and smiled into the applause which had been loud and long with the skinny kids jumping up and down and whistling so shrilly that it hurt Fishbait's ears just to remember it. The big Jap touched his elbow and smiled, motioning with a nod of the head toward the three Seminoles now struggling to get the gator back into its tub.

"Take picture? Of a me over there?" But a clot of people had gotten in between them and Fishbait found himself being propelled toward the exit, the head of a fat lady pressing into his bad arm and one of the skinny kids bumping into his side each time he took a step. Marc Potter had been sitting to one side of the entrance to a roped-off tent when Fishbait finally broke free of the crowd and stopped. Snakes of all colors and sizes were painted on the sides of the tent, intertwined and coiled so densely that it was impossible to follow any one of them from nose to tip.

"You can just go on in, Mr. Johnson. No charge."

"What is it?"

"Reptile show. Snakes mostly. Got some big ones in there."

"What kind?"

"All kinds." Marc's smile had been much like that of a patient parent trying hard not to be irritated by the repeated failure of a child to master some simple chore. Fishbait began to smile back but Marc's expression had changed, becoming almost neutral with just a touch of humor about the eyes. "We have almost every species here."

"Where do they come from—the rattlers?" The line of people had moved quickly through the opening in the tent, the last of them craning their necks to see what lay ahead. Fishbait could still hear the whirring clicks of cameras and the excited squeals of children seemingly layered among the deeper noises of the crowd as it waited for whatever was coming to begin. Marc had nodded toward the tent.

"We have our own farms. The rattlers are mostly from the one in Mississippi. Go on in and enjoy the show."

"What do they do in there?"

"It's mostly educational. Teaches about snakes."

"Like in school?" Fishbait had tried to picture what it might look like inside but nothing would stay long enough to be studied. He already had decided not to go himself. "Like that?"

"Not exactly. Go and see for yourself. You get to touch snakes. See them up close. That kind of thing. You ever touch a snake, Mr. Johnson?"

"Yes sir." He had remembered the seven foot rattler he had battled that one time down near the preacher's house, his catching-pole and special sack the Institute had given him barely strong enough to hold all the power that came boiling up from the hot sand near the palmetto thicket like a killer wave in a hurricane. That one had whipped its tail four times across his legs before being twisted into the sack and tied off. "I hunt 'em."

But Marc hadn't seemed to hear as he stood up and stretched. Walking quickly to the tent flap, he began to lower it slowly, pulling back at one point and motioning toward Fishbait to go inside. The big Jap had suddenly appeared behind Marc and tapped softly on his shoulder.

"What?"

"Sir? Is too rate to go inside?" He noticed Fishbait and smiled broadly.

"You come too?"

And Fishbait had walked over and followed the Jap inside before even starting to think any more about not wanting to do it. Marc had patted him twice on the shoulder and let down the flap, blocking out the sunlight and leaving Fishbait beside the Jap on the last row of benches trying hard to make out what was happening in the circle of light twenty rows ahead. He had tried to listen to the Jap but the loudspeakers blotted out all sound but the deep voice of Buck Potter who stood on a raised platform to one side. Fishbait had never seen so many snakes as he saw stacked up in glass boxes set against the far walls of the tent like half-finished building blocks some giant toymaker had let sit until morning.

James L. Fortuna, Jr.

And it was then that he had felt the sickness in his belly, like now and like it felt the time his uncle took him deep into the woods to find the dancing people, their eyes like corpses but their bodies not yet allowed to fall down to rest. And every one held snakes, his uncle holding two once he had joined the dance, but Fishbait ran into the brush and hid and watched it all until the sickness hit, his belly throbbing with the pain, each wave of it cut stronger than the last until there was no way to hold them in. The earth had felt cool against his cheek but still he watched; even as he heaved, he watched as one and two and three went stiff and let go of the snakes and fell down on their knees to sing or shout out words he couldn't understand. And then he had come back to the semi-darkness of the tent and felt more than he saw the rising shape and presence of a thing he now believed he never should have gone to see, a power there no longer safely locked in memory or in dreams, no longer fearing even poles and singing in the air and sunlight warm across its hunter's back. But last Sunday the big Jap had nudged him with an elbow and turned to help a young woman in a cowboy suit unwrap the thick, dark coils that lapped around her arm. Fishbait twisted on his bed and shut his eyes and made the dancing streaks of sunlight go away. It was good to stay at home and let his belly rest.

A Season of Dwarfs

The spring his parents left with the Colonel Waller Shows, Jim Canaan turned ten. His father had begun building a tinsel-starred and glittered house-like structure on the bed of the cattle truck months before he got it to chug and rattle and sway down the clay road, last vehicle in a caravan, moving through the still, cool darkness toward the main road and the beginning of another season. Jim's parents had met years before, traveling in the same shows and gradually coming together, at first in partnership as co-owners of an almost overlooked ring-toss game and then, married, as owners of a barely more successful fortune-telling booth, until finally leaving the road altogether and settling down in Seacrest County, Florida, on the farm of his grandmother. Whenever he thought of the last time he saw his parents, during a springtime particularly moist and heavy-scented, drenched it seemed in rose and white camellia, he thought mostly of the dwarfs and their pig-like dog, Tippy, and the pasture behind the barn where the carnival camped.

The first dwarf had appeared the morning after the show rolled in, a frayed and tattered line of sputter-popping parodies of cars and trucks which overwhelmed even the skreeking sounds of the nearby swamp and came to rest finally in the center of a neglected pasture. Jim had watched it all from the front porch until the moon was full in the sky toward Stone Crab Beach and the kerosene stoves and lanterns were glowing through the semi-darkness of the pasture like so many coals in among the ashes of a dying campfire. His grandmother had come up behind him so quietly that he jumped back into the wall when she touched his shoulder.

"Best get on to bed. Them folks'll be up too late for you."

"Why're they here?"

"Ask your Pa and Mama. They the ones goin' off with them." And despite all the obvious signs of moving, the building on the truck and the repairing of trunks and suitcases nearly worn through from rough handling, it was not until his grandmother had spoken the words that Jim could begin to form in his mind the actual act itself, could almost see his father wave or his mother smile before they stepped through the tall grass of the pasture and were lost to sight behind a delicate curtain of lantern or stove light.

"But why?"

"Ask them yourself."

"What about me?"

"Stayin' here. They say they'll be back for you."

"What d'you say?"

"I say you best learn a trade and stay free of the road."

During the night, at some point when the black was so deep that it seemed it could be touched or held in the hand, he had heard a grunting bark outside his window. But sleep had pulled him back from the sound, almost immediately, and it seemed only minutes until his room was awash in the misted light of dawn. At first he thought the shape he saw framed by curtains was one of his grandmother's cactus plants, somehow moved during the night from its spot in a corner of the front porch and balanced precariously on the narrow ledge of his bedroom window. But this cactus had been topped by a baseball cap and spoke in a raspy tone, individual words interspersed with slow whistles and clucks.

"Hey there. Is yer awake? Ain't seen no dog has yer?" For a moment he had thought he was dreaming, listening to words filtered through distorted speakers as they came at him heavy and bloated like the carcass of a dead possum bumping into the grassy bank of a swamp island. He had sat up and rubbed his eyes.

"Has yer seen a dog or not?" The cactus rose up a bit, just above the window ledge, and Jim could make out an orange shirt and a bright red bow-tie.

"Does yer talk?"

"Yes."

"Ah, good. I'm Manny an' I'm out lookin' for my dog. Has yer seen her?"

"No."

"Well. Maybe she got on home. Thank yer."

At breakfast, he had wanted to tell his parents about the cactus but they seemed not to hear him as they noisily ate his grandmother's pancakes and talked about packing the truck.

"You got them trunks ready?"

"Last night."

"Pa, this morning I seen this—"

"You two are foolish. At your ages. You got this child here now."

"It's only for the season, Ma. We'll be back as soon as th'season's over."

"Momma, this cactus was—"

"I know you Josh Canaan. I know you an' nothin' don't change." And then the cactus was outside the screen door behind Jim's father, red baseball cap, bright orange shirt, red bow tie and all as he knocked on the facing. Jim's father turned around.

"Hey—it's Manny! C'mon in here boy."

"Thank yer." Jim's grandmother sniffed and turned back to her pancakes as Manny opened the door and wobbled into the room, his bandied legs arcing down into oversized shoes that squeaked as he walked.

"C'mon an' sit down—right here. Billie's going out to th'camp anyways." Jim's mother had smiled and pushed out from the table. The cactus nodded his head.

"Thank yer. Josh'a, them smell like pancakes."

"Ma—can we have—"

"Pa—this here's the cactus I—" And then a girl cactus had appeared in the doorway, hair bouncing on her shoulders each time she tapped her long fingernails on the tight screening.

"Sandy! Damn, Manny—whole family here?"

"All but Tippy—dog has run off, Josh'a." Sandy bobbed up into the chair next to Jim, his grandmother's chair, and folded flipper-like hands on the table. She looked over at Jim and smiled.

"You haven't seen a dog, have you?"

"No ma'am. What's he look like?"

"You'd know her. She's part pig." Jim's grandmother snorted, almost a chuckle-like sound and one of the pancakes flopped over onto the floor.

"Yer dropped one, ma'am. Did yer see it?" Manny's eyes widened as he spoke the words, eyebrows arching and his mouth squinching up with each movement of his lips. Jim's grandmother turned around slowly, the wooden spatula held firmly before her like a battered scepter. Jim's father had visibly winced and seemed to be trying to decide if he should raise his hands.

"I seen it mister—mister? Your friend here got a name, Josh—or only a mouth?"

"Manny, Ma. Manny and Sandy. They're with the show."

"I done figured out that much. They got a last name?" The tip of the spatula circled tightly in the now smoky air of the kitchen.

"Pancakes burnin', Ma?"

"Lordy!" She swung back to the stove, looking to Jim like one of the mechanical bell-ringers he had seen in a department store window last Christmas. And then he turned to watch Manny, staring closely as he could at the reddened skin, in places seeming to have been folded carelessly like he himself sometimes did with his sheets and blanket on school mornings when he had overslept. He still looked like a cactus, tiny wire-like hairs protruding at odd angles from within the folds of his skin or the smoother places on his neck and flippers. Sandy noticed Jim and smiled.

"He yours, Joshua?"

"Yeah—Jim—Jim, this here's Sandy."

"Ma'am." He had noticed her lips were painted deep red, cardinal-colored, and she licked the slender tip of her tongue over them as she talked. She had moved her chair closer to Manny by the time Grandmother dropped the tin of pancakes down dangerously close to the molasses can resting near Jim's outstretched hand.

"Pancakes ain't no good cold." She stepped to the pantry and almost without a pause gathered up plates, silverware, and cups—finally piling them on the nearby counter. "Help yourself to a plate. Coffee's on th'stove. I got work to do." And she was gone amid a flutter of skirts and a few well-placed stomps on the hallway side of the kitchen door. Jim's father's words came out all low and raspy and slow.

"Get some plates an' forks for these people, Jim." As a dog tried to bark outside, Jim watched the two cactuses wink at each other and touch heads and finally hold flipper-hands, plump skin pressing into each other and making them almost indistinguishable. At the door, a short and bloated dog pressed its snout into the rusty screen and flicked its tongue in and out over the rough surface.

"Hey there—will yer look? Tippy's out there." Manny's flippers closed on the top pancake. Outside, the dog began a grunting sound, its tongue still rubbing over the screen and lips curled back into a jagged smile which reminded Jim of an old gator who sunned himself in the short reeds down near the abandoned sawmill.

"More pancakes for yer, Jimmy boy?" Manny's eyes were opened wide, pushed back into a ridge of bulged and wrinkled skin beneath which bushy eyebrows helped his face look locked in deep surprise. The dog had disappeared.

"No thank you."

-ii-

The camp in the pasture seemed almost to have sprung up unaided from the short grass and wild flowers, its tents and lean-tos and hastily erected shacks all colored with the intensity of the earliest vegetation of spring. Up ahead, Colonel Waller's trailer was painted in deep reds and blues, thick thunderbolts sweeping in alternating colors down both sides of it, and a shallow deck seeming to have been jammed into its back like a forklift digging under a packing crate. The Colonel sat beneath a frayed umbrella as dark wisps of smoke curled into the clear air above the row of midway tents that stretched before him almost to the north fence. Jim watched his father's back, walking close behind him as he maneuvered easily among people and equipment better suited to the bright screen of a movie theatre than the greening pasture of a truck and dairy farm. Jim had glanced a few times side to side, seeing first Manny balancing Sandy on a seat stuck atop a thick pole, and then another cactus, a plump black one feeding a baby in the entrance of a darkened tent. She had winked at Jim and pursed her lips as if to blow him a kiss, which made the tips of his ears begin to burn like the first jolt of a bee sting. But his father had spoken to her first, claiming the gesture for himself.

"Myra—where's Colonel?"

"In his trailer, JC. Colonel been there since sunup. Lookin' at the peoples, I reckon. Nobody know what the Colonel look at."

"Girl this time, Myra?"

"Naw. 'nother boy. I got three now. Two looks like they goin' grow. I can use th' lil' one, though. Manny thinks he'll do jus' fine. You goin' out this time, JC?"

"Yeah. But just for the season."

"Uh huh, I hear ya. Boy there goin' too?"

"No. Jim's stayin' with Ma. It's just a season."

"Uh huh."

And then they moved on, shuffling at times toward the trailer which came to rise above the surrounding vehicles and tents like some mute sentinel set down to guard what nobody else wanted. It took Jim until almost the front steps of the Colonel's deck to notice that all the people they had passed were cactus-like, whirls of varied colors and skin tones and stages of undress. Even the taller people appeared stooped, as if somehow persuaded to disguise their true height and try to blend in as best they could with the jumble of moving cactuses which made the collection of tents seem alive with the kind of energy Jim had only seen ants show in pulling food inside their hills. He had wanted to ask his father about it all, but before he could think of the right words to use they both were standing at the edge of a wooden deck looking up at a medium-sized cactus in a cowboy hat around whose rough face cigar smoke curled like strands of thick rope.

"Colonel, I want you to meet—" The cactus had held up a pudgy index finger and slowly stood up, cowboy boots catching first on the last rung of his chair before being put firmly down on the rough planks of the deck. The voice sounded like it was being forced through water, various syllables spraying out into the air like droplets spinning off the roof of a wet and speeding car.

"Minute. Smiffie! Smiffie—come h'ar!" A stoop-shouldered man slowly approached the deck glancing from side to side above him like a turtle. The cactus turned toward him, head cocked and eyes seeming to bulge a bit as he spoke again. "You want something, Smiffie?"

"Colonel, Manny—Manny said—said—" The man seemed to be trying to hide behind one of the deck poles. "He—He—wanted me to ask—to ask—"

"Ast what, Smiffie? What does Manny want?"

"The—the risers—risers—Manny wanted to know what we—what we should do with them." The last words came out all in a rush, seeming to bunch up and collide with each other, and the man's head bowed even lower.

"Rithers? Rithers? Did you say, rithers, boy? Was that it?

"Yes—yes—he wanted to know what to do with them, Colonel—where—what—"

"Schtow the damn rithers—pack 'em up—pack 'em all up—you hear?"

"Now, Colonel—should we do it now or wait until—"

"Yeath by—God forgive me—Jesuth—now! We leavin' at dawn." And then the Colonel turned to Jim and his father and raised one eyebrow, cigar smoke now furiously whirling about his ear. The turtle-looking man had disappeared. "Jothua—you bring your father with you?" jutting the stubby cigar out in the general direction of Jim. From somewhere behind them, bells sounded, shrill and faintly out of tune as if discordant pitches had been purposely joined together in a wind chime. The Colonel positioned the cigar more firmly in the corner of his mouth and tried to smile.

"Jim, this here's Colonel C.D. Waller." Jim's dad bent over and tugged Jim closer to the deck.

"Boy. You goin' out with uth?" The smoke cleared and Jim stared fascinated at the Colonel's lips, plump and wide and tinged with a red much like his mother used on Sundays when Grandmother succeeded in worrying them all up from bed and down the road to Meeting. Jim wanted to leave his father and the Colonel and walk among the tents and try to find a pig-like dog.

"Your boy talk, Jothua?"

"Answer Colonel, son." Jim had never seen his father act that way, not exactly frightened but near trembling in his hands and bowed head and his voice cracking mid-sentence like those of the older boys at school. The Colonel held the cigar between two ringed fingers and had begun smacking his fat lips together by the time Jim spoke, his own words seeming to have been dropped into a well and made into echoes as they tried to climb the distance to the deck.

"I heard this thing last night, Pa. Outside. And then this morning—at my window, there was—"

The Colonel smiled and winked at Jim's father. To one side, Jim could see Manny and Sandy tumbling together with three others, grass bending under them each time they sat down and thrust up a leg or arm, moving like a disjointed caterpillar down the ragged midway toward the deck, only to veer off two tents away and disappear behind a red trailer parked near a row of neatly stacked risers.

"Boy didn't sleep much last night, Colonel. All excited 'bout the show comin' in."

"You fixthed up, Jothua? All thigned up?"

"Yes sir. Last night. We're ready but for packin' th'truck."

"Your missuth able?"

"She's ready, Colonel. Been practicing palms an' cards an' tea leaves on me th'past two months."

"Pa, it talked to me."

"Your boy talkths right well, Jothua."

"Hush now, Jim." He had seemed on the verge of reaching out for his son's mouth, fingers starting to stretch toward him before being stopped abruptly and jammed quickly into the side pockets of his pea-jacket. "Boy must of dreamed somethin' last night, Colonel."

"It weren't no dream, Pa. I seen it this mornin'. Two of 'em. You remember. And that dog was outside? What are they, Pa. I seen more of 'em here." The Colonel puffed hard on his cigar and rubbed a hand slowly along the rail, his eyes narrowing as he stood on tiptoe and stared hard and carefully down past Joshua's shoulder as if noticing Jim for the first time.

"What you suppoth he'th talking about?"

"Cactus."

"You say cactuth, boy?" The Colonel's teeth closed tightly on the cigar and his eyes bulged slightly as he looked from son to father and finally settled himself more firmly on the deck, fingers now tapping on the rail.

"Colonel, the boy has been—"

"Cachtuth?"

"Yes sir. Cactus. Only they ain't, I guess. I mean, I know they ain't." Manny and the others reappeared briefly, slightly behind and to the right of the Colonel's trailer, before missing a connection and all scattering among various tents and cars. A taller cactus was juggling several oranges near where Manny lay stretched out, pushing Sandy away as she tried to get him to balance her on his knees.

"Colonel, the boy don't know about this show. I ain't never told him. Go on, Jim. Walk around. I'll find you later. Go on and look around."

"You there—boy!"

"Yes sir?"

"What you think *I* look like?" Jim stared at the Colonel carefully, slowly moving his eyes from the tips of his well-tooled boots to the feathery Stetson cocked severely down over one eye. The bells sounded again, this time seeming to parody a toy xylophone being dropped downstairs.

"A milk can—but I know you ain't."

-iii-

Jim had not stopped running until he reached a bare spot of ground near the salt-lick. He hadn't looked back as he dodged tent lines and dust-covered cars and trucks, letting the almost squeal-like shouts of the Colonel and the lower-pitched calls of his father chase after him always a safe distance behind. He kicked the moist dirt, digging his boot toe into the spongy ridges left by the cattle as they attacked the salt. The day was getting warmer, clouds giving way to a sunlight which at times hurt his eyes as he stared at the flashy sides of the tinseled tents a few yards away. The camp was still awash in pre-dawn mist, steam and cook-fire smoke blending and rising into the cloudless sky like the semi-transparent curtains he had seen in the movies, drawn downward by unseen hands to provide temporary privacy for lovers or spies. He didn't want his parents to leave with the Colonel, to drive off down the road behind a milk-can and more cactus than he had ever seen in his life. He turned toward the house and began to wave at what he thought was his grandmother. But the sky passed by his feet, whirling past him in a progression soon broken by dirt ridges and a glimpse of salt-lick and barbed wire and tent and finally eyes which blinked at him as he sat on two oversized shoes and felt his stomach churn pancakes and molasses. The cactus had come out to play.

"Did yer like that?" He could only glimpse Manny's face behind him, stubby flippers bent and clasped somehow behind his neck. He pushed one and then the other of Jim's buttocks with the tips of his shoes, as if trying to decide whether to drop him into the moist dirt or toss him over to Sandy. "Did yer?"

"I ain't never done that before." Jim watched Sandy's eyes wrinkle up and her laughter sounded much like the bells he had heard earlier as he watched the Colonel puff out smoke from his stubby cigar. Others had gathered around, some fatter than Manny and Sandy and some a bit taller, some in hats and some bareheaded, but all recognizable as cactus-people, with fuzzy skin that seemed to catch the sunlight in ways that made them glow. "Best let me down. My Grandma's calling me."

"We'nt heard her. Any gramma calls?" Manny's voice seemed aimed first at the circle of cactus and then directly into Jim's back. "Did yer like it?"

"I guess." Jim tried to look as closely as possible at Sandy's flippers, studying their rings and deeply colored tips. But she suddenly dropped down, sitting at first and then on her back, feet upraised as she clapped her ankles together and prepared to catch a momentarily flying Jim.

"Hey—stop!" But the laughter drowned out his words as he passed back and forth between them, fearing each time that one of them would miss and leave him to crash head or backside first into the barbed wire of the nearby fence. "Stop!" And then the sky and dirt spun by again and he felt himself leave the wobbly security of Manny's shoes.

"Put out yer feet!" And he landed beyond the bare spot, momentum carrying him forward at a half-run, legs finally buckling and the grass coming up to cushion his fall. Raising himself up on one elbow, he looked over at the cactus-people and bit his lip.

"Are yer all right, Jimmy boy?" Manny's smile revealed a gold front tooth and a missing lower one. A wide dog wobbled out from the middle of the other cactus, grunting as it walked, sounding like someone were squeezing its sides with each step it took on legs seemingly too slender to bear up its bloated torso. The dog came close, sniffed a few times almost nostril-level with Jim, and then licked its lips with a tongue that looked mismatched with the hog-like appearance of its snout. "Tippy wants to make friends with yer."

"I want to go home." He had felt on the verge of not so much tears as the dry sobbing which sometimes made him wake up at night and wonder where he was, dreams having taken him far away, following his parents and trying to find them in one after another of the places they had told him of in bedtime stories or front-porch talk or casual mention on Saturday drives to town. But nowhere had there been cactus-people and talking milk-cans and dogs that looked like one of Grandma's pigs.

"Where's your papa, Jimmy?" Sandy had smiled, squatted down and tilted her head, watching him like the dog itself, now fuzzy snout forward and one ear slightly angled to the right. "Is he with Colonel?"

"Yes." He tried to see beyond the circle of cactus, to the fence and past it over the scrub grass and palmetto to the front porch and Grandma. But they wouldn't let him, their clothes blocking his view and forcing him to look into Sandy's eyes. And then her flippers seemed to have closed on his shoulders even before he noticed their movement, and her roll backward seemed to pull his stomach into his throat as her knees lifted him up and passed him into the suddenly outstretched arms or prickly flippers of the other cactus-people, Manny central to all their swinging until one last heave tossed Jim over the barbed wire into a mound of steaming manure on the house side of the fence. In the distance, he could see a thin stream of smoke curling up from the kitchen chimney and below, in the deep shade of the front porch, a shape like his grandmother shaking out blankets. The cactus-people were staring at him, a line of smiling faces just above the top strand of wire. He felt like crying as he stood up and wiped at his clothes. "I didn't like it."

Manny rubbed his chin with a glistening flipper-hand and glanced toward the midway. The others began to wobble back toward sounds of calliope music and motor-crackle and a distant rumbled chorus of shrill voices, rat-like at times yet buffered by the tinseled canvas of accumulated seasons. But it had been Sandy who spoke first, checking her makeup in the mirror of a silver dollar-sized compact.

"Get the dog, Manny." Manny stooped down and rested his face near Tippy's head, contented grunts mingling with the by then almost crystalline music and shrill murmuring of the midway. The words seemed to be coming from the dog's snout, its eyes red-tinged in the approaching noontime.

"Hast yer seen a little man anywheres?" Above them, Sandy giggled and dabbed at her lips with delicate fingers.

The Gator and the Holy Ghost

Whenever he thought back on the day itself, an afternoon matinee that had been suddenly canceled and then
just as suddenly rescheduled, the Reverend Billy Manatee
still wondered at the complete surprise of it all and mostly
at his own lack of preparation for what the voice said to him
and what he had been told to do. It had been typical late
summer weather, hot and damp and a northeastern Florida
sky with tall clouds out toward the ocean resembling columns of un-ginned cotton bolls pasted onto a slowly moving bolt of pale blue cloth. He had liked the heat then, and
the way sweat had made his dark skin glisten even before
he stepped into the water and waded the few feet, waist
deep, over to the low box cages holding whichever of the
bull gators Colonel Foster wanted the people to see sleeping belly up in the sunshine. But that last day it had been a
new gator, fresh from its home deep in Sutter's Swamp, an
untested and red-eyed addition to the thirty or so veterans
of the Ponta Gorda Institute's summer shows, an eventual
ten-foot blur of thick ridges and deep hisses that made Billy
feel a touch of cold spread out over him in spite of the blinking ninety-five degrees on the nearby electric thermometer.
At first, the gator had seemed asleep, the tip of its snout
pushing into the sliding mesh door of its box, just a few

small side teeth visible at close range. That had been over twenty years ago and yet the feel of the water and the weight of the battle had never left him.

The breeze felt cool as he sat down on the front steps of the church and watched a tractor-trailer roll by out on the dusty road that rimmed his property like a black necklace on a fat lady's neck, dipping and rising and occasionally lost to sight altogether behind a sweep of bulged greenery that marked the beginning of the long curve toward town. He loved to sit out in the early afternoon, especially in the fall when the heat was tempered with shafts of cooler air that made his skin feel awkward, tingled and calm by turns. Beyond the gravel of the walkway out front, a male cardinal swept his wings against the air and gently touched down atop the church sign, the dark wood sparkling in the October sunlight and giving its red lettering a hint of motion. He had carved the sign himself ten years before, in cypress and walnut, putting it in place out there on the fifteenth anniversary of his ordination.

FIERY DOVE FELLOWSHIP
Divine Healing Center
FULL GOSPEL
Services: Sunday 10:00 and 6:00
Wed. 6:00
Pastor: Rev. Billy Manatee

Billy stretched out his legs, letting the heels of his loafers press into the edge of the grass near the bottom step. Wednesday service was in two hours and the sounds of his wife's practicing behind him in the semi-darkness of the sanctuary made him smile. Maybelle's fiddle notes at times seemed to rise up and pause and then tumble over each other after a tune progression both sad and triumphant, a momentary link with the Pentecostal circuit she had moved along in one band or another until finishing up as his wife just in time to get him properly baptized and enrolled in Saratoga Springs Bible College. The songs were sometimes painfully shrill, their teenaged daughters calling them "nose music," and Maybelle seldom played that way for the church. But all that had come long after that one day in the greenish water of the gator tank with a bleacher's worth of paying customers drinking pop and maybe swatting at sand flies and looking down at a young, half-Seminole, flat-bellied then and trying hard to coax an untested gator out of its box. The fiddle left off sawing at memories and settled itself into a version of "Blow a Trumpet in Zion." Traffic out on the road began picking up, a sign of shift changes at the mills. The cardinal flew away in a blur of red. Billy closed his eyes and let the sunshine hold his body, slight paunch pressing into the cloth of his blue shirt and his tie moving sideways with his breathing.

Maybelle had been there that one day, both prologue and epilogue to the matinee, red cowboy boots and crane legs showing beneath a blue jumper and a peach-colored blouse whose spangles caught the sun like tiny explosions of light being set off one at a time. She had been playing at the nearby fairgrounds, at some variety of all day or night gospel sing where the audience slept in campers or pitched tents to save on money and be sure of staying safe among others of their own kind. He had been resting nearby in a thatch-roofed dressing room (a place the Colonel had set up for him)—mostly open-air but with a cot there and just enough privacy to change clothes and maybe nap. Not long after he stretched out on the cot, drowsy, and nearly asleep, Little Jesse had come on duty and started the crowd through the turnstiles out front, moving his arms like a tired shepherd who has lost his crook and dogs, eyes most likely already the shade of unfocussed red they took on whenever he was late to work and the Colonel caught him at it. Jesse's voice suddenly had gone up about three notches, a few people seeming to jump through the turnstiles as he flapped his arms out to his sides like a wounded pelican. Billy had given up on a nap and decided instead to check on Jesse. By then, Maybelle's angry voice was rising up clearly through all the crowd noises and Jesse's slightly nasal piping. She had looked angry too, skinny legs seeming to rise up out of her boots with each word she spoke like they were somehow connected together by wire.

"No rats, lady. You can't have no kind a pets in here."

"This ain't a rat."

"Yes it is too a rat, lady. And it ain't going in."

By the time Billy walked over to the gate, the rest of the people had already passed through. Only Maybelle and Jesse were left, standing close together, Jesse's long nose pointing down in a bulged arch toward Maybelle's upturned face like a shotgun trained on some crook he had caught and didn't know what to do with. Billy's vest had been the same color as Maybelle's jumper, a dark blue, but his with a fanned peacock on the back that his mother had embroidered waiting for someone to notice the Indian dolls and beadwork she tried to sell three days a week at the bus depot back home in Welaka. But Maybelle hadn't seemed to notice anything but Jesse's nose and the words that he kept pushing out at her as he began to back up against the turnstiles. He sounded near rage level, a slight quivering in his voice that Billy had heard only a few times before.

"You ain't taking that rat in here, lady."

"It ain't no rat."

"Dammit, lady—that thing's a rat." Seeing Billy standing nearby, Jesse had shifted his weight and wedged his hips in between the counter box and a thick turnstile spoke. His arms were crossed on his chest and the nose had begun to dip and rise like it had taken on an existence all its own.

"Billy—look here. C'mere." Up close his eyes were nearly all red, only a few streaks of white visible in them and the skin to either side splotched in purplish welts. And then Maybelle's face had come into focus, still clear in memory even after twenty-five years, a delicate contrast in dark and pale with almost crow-black hair and skin so smooth-looking that Billy had thought she was wearing a porcelain mask. "Billy—lookit this," Jesse waved a shaking hand in the general direction of Maybelle's chest, "just lookit this damn thing here and tell me what you see."

But before Billy could answer, the loudspeakers had already begun crackling out the music Colonel Foster insisted on hearing before every show, an indistinctive medley of show tunes and Sousa marches that gradually spilled itself into a whirling thump of drum solos, vaguely African in their beat and tempo. Maybelle had tapped her boot toe and kept staring at Jesse. Billy licked his lips and half-smiled.

"What's going on?"

He had not been prepared for the intensity of Maybelle's eyes, her face seeming to turn away from Jesse's so quickly that he felt himself pulled into her problem even before she fully noticed he was there at all. She had patted at a ball of fur protruding from one side of her jumper and seemed to be waiting for exactly the right word. But Jesse spoke first.

"Claims this here ain't a rat, Billy." He had uncrossed his arms and grabbed hold of either side of the turnstile, body still forming a barrier and nose now seeming to twitch as he spoke. "I told her Colonel don't let no pets in here, Billy." His voice took on a pleading quality, eyes now blinking and his hands almost fluttering against the sides of his pants.

"He's right, Miss. That's the rule." And Billy had smiled his best smile, consciously making his teeth show and letting his own eyes nearly lose themselves in the tanned wrinkles of skin puckering up and out just above his cheeks. It had always worked before. But Maybelle didn't seem to notice how hard he was trying.

"And like I told him, Mister—this," she patted again at the ball of fur, "ain't no rat."

"Does look like one though, Miss." Billy had liked the way she bit at her lower lip and how her bare knees twitched as she rested her weight on one leg. Her voice was growing softer, individual words at times difficult to hear above the drum-beats coming out through one of the nearby speakers. It was almost time for Billy to go into the water. "Or like a Mexican Chihuahua." He had taken a step closer. "Too hairy though." He kept smiling, his eyes nearly level with hers, calculating that she would be a half-head shorter or more without her boots.

She wore a gold cross around her neck, dangling down into the spangles to one side of the ball of fur, the chain caught on a shiny paw that the closer he came to it, the less real it looked, plastic-like and dead. Jesse had stepped free of the turnstile as Maybelle reached up and unclipped the ball of fur, tugging its paw loose from the chain and smoothing down its pointed ears and finally smiling at Billy.

"See—it ain't no rat. Now can I get in there? I already paid, y'know?" The smile flickered and went away and it was only later, after his time in the water with the gator and the voice at intervals so blended that it seemed voice and gator were one and the same, that he had sat across the table from her in the tiny oyster bar down on Timaquan Inlet, watching the smile grow stronger and stronger and trying to understand the words she spoke:

"No—that wasn't a mistake. That was the power of the Holy Ghost and He don't make mistakes."

But the fight had come first, even now in memory clean-etched and unlike any of the ones that had come before, different even from the moment he had stood there in the water reaching out to undo the latch and signal one of the pool boys to pull up the mesh gate and prod the gator outside and into a glide toward the dry dock and wrestling island a few yards away.

Listening to the momentarily ragged bowing behind him in the sanctuary, Billy closed his eyes and saw again, almost as clearly as viewing it on a TV screen, the wagging movement of the gator's thick tail as it parted the greenish water, causing a line of froth to lap up against Billy's thighs and the sides of the other boxes, the gator's snout at first just inches away from his outstretched hands until in a quick movement his fingers clamped down hard, fingers pressing into the surprisingly soft skin under the jaw and then a push with his hip and the gator was caught in what the Colonel called the dry dock, a narrow channel cut into the island that spilled into a shallower pool just a few feet away from the padded table where the gator finally would sleep, belly up and fat legs slightly quivering in the sunshine. He had done it scores of times, losing count after his third season when the Colonel had put in the matinee and hired extra help. And Billy had been the best, Chief Billy who came from the barely tolerant stares of classmates at Flagler High to stage center and the applause of people from as far away as Japan. The Institute's crowds loved him and the Colonel had not discouraged his decision to drop out of school and go to work full-time.

"Do what you do, Billy. You'll always have work here."

"But what about off-season?"

"You're the best, Billy. Best I ever seen. We'll work it out." And he had, finding things for him to do and keeping the pay coming until even Billy's mother had seemed to give over her disappointment and let up on her attempts to get him saved and back in school. The old woman loved him but never understood the gators.

"But you'll need school for later. For when you can't fight no more. Your father went to college."

"And left us, Ma. Left us down there with no help from nobody."

"You need school."

"I got me a good job, Ma."

"Well, you still need Jesus—you can't say that you don't need Him."

"I got the Colonel, Ma."

"That ain't nothing!"

But it had been enough for almost five years, years in which he had worked hard and sent half his paycheck down to Welaka and felt good about what he was doing until one letter came back and his brother showed up at the Institute a few days later and told him how she died.

"She went fast, Billy. A week ago."

"Why didn't you call me?"

"Didn't know how. She said to give you this." Her Bible had been wrapped in Frosty the Snowman paper, covered by scenes of a sitting, smiling Frosty and a jumping Frosty and finally a dancing Frosty, top hat held in one fat fist high up over his head while cartoon-like children bounced along after him or rolled in the snow or just stood on water-stained snow banks watching it all happen. Billy had taken a long time unwrapping it, for some reason saving the paper and only later opening the Bible itself and reading the childish scrawl that covered almost the full page before Genesis. He still had it, cover now smooth and torn in service as his pulpit guide, but back when it had come free of Frosty and his friends it seemed a poor repayment for all those checks.

> *Read it everday*
> *and let it be your gide.*

Love everbody and wate upon the Lard.

And yet that gift had come back to him a year later, his mother's words breaking out clear as day at the exact moment that gator had decided to tear loose from the dry dock and take both of them headfirst into the shallow pool beneath the wrestling table.

> *The joy of the Lard is your strength.*
> *Never forget to pray and wate on the Lard*
> *to gide your fotesteps.*

From the little he could remember hearing, the crowd had started whooping louder than the Colonel could make his voice come out over the speakers. And then as the green water had closed over his head and the gator's body jerked sideways to press itself between his legs and begin to buck like some kind of rodeo mustang, he knew he hadn't even wanted to open that last gift, had wanted instead to forget it was there at all, rewrapped in Frosty and taking up a corner in his footlocker back in the trailer the Colonel had bought him his third year out. But when he broke surface, straddling the gator's back with aching fingers still clamped down on its jaw and legs pressing in to keep them both from rolling any more into the frothed mess of a pool, he knew that the book was coming back on him in a way even stronger than when his mother had been around to talk about what it said and what it could help him do, her words until then never seeming as real to him as the bare fact of his father's desertion and the feel of a gator being muscled onto dry land and put to sleep while a crowd of strangers yelled themselves hoarse.

The gator suddenly had interrupted his thinking, taking away his mother's words and the presence of the book by

swatting out its tail and splintering the rim of the dry dock
and bringing in a flood of water from the main pool and taking him again head-first into a deeper green. For a moment
he could hear people shouting above him close at hand
and a pressure of fingers on his shoulders but they were
soon lost to the thrashing sounds of the water and wood
and crackle of the Colonel's voice each time a roll brought
him into the air and all of it covered by the hissing of the
gator as it tried to get its teeth free from Billy's fingers. He
had kept thinking of the book as he rolled, its cover genuine
leather and the gold of its lettering deeply etched and bold-
looking, the H and B in Holy Bible seeming then in memory
tall enough to stretch a hammock between and the print
something he wanted to dive into and rub all over his aching muscles and let inside his brain to stop the howling that
was strengthening each time the gator tried a new roll or
buck or twisting dive. And just before the long rest on the
bottom, he saw Maybelle's face, eyes pleading with him to
do or say something that she alone knew how while her
own mouth pushed out words he ached to hear and give
back to her, much like his lungs and head came to ache
down there under the green waiting for the gator to catch its
second wind and try to take them both right through the
rubber of the pool's bottom perhaps to tumble and roll together, over and over, until nobody could reach wherever it
was they finally came to rest. But only the gator had been
there to hear the words that came into him after he managed somehow to cry out for help within the green darkness, bubbles whirling around his face from the effort it took
to push it outside.

"Oh my God—"

And the voice that answered was free of bubbles and seemed strong enough to shut the gator's eyes and keep it still and quiet and incapable of diving deeper.

BOY—WHAT ARE YOU DOING?

He had started to answer with his mouth but found little air left to make the words come through his teeth, to free up what his brain was screaming out in a cadence and tempo close-linked with that of his pounding heart, and all that finally did push clear was a blub-blub whooshing noise, a limp plop-plop that bubbled upward to where he was certain the sun still shown and the crowd still cheered. The gator seemed asleep beneath his legs, ridged back motionless and invisible in the center of the green down near the distant bottom of the pool.

BOY—BOY DO YOU HEAR ME?

A swirl of blub-blub must have touched the voice, giving it what it wanted to hear or at least encouraging it enough to ask for more.

YOU ARE A MESS, BOY. DO YOU LIKE BEING A MESS?

But it had been the gator who answered, talking in its sleep in spite of Billy's fingers still pressed down tightly on its snout, tiny bubbles streaming out its nose in the play of words more felt than heard.

"The show must go on."

And then the voice came down around them both, Billy and the gator, with a force that popped them to the surface, nearly emptying the pool like an apple dropped into a cup full of coffee.

THE SHOW IS MINE, BOY. GET YOURSELF OUT OF THAT WATER AND FIND A BETTER WAY.

There had been people up there, many of them, the Colonel himself pulling Billy free of the gator with his big hands feeling like pinchers as he pried fingers loose from the hide of its lower snout, and even Little Jesse helping bring down the heavy catching net to make the separation complete. But the voice hadn't stopped the whole time, seeming to build in power as the water let go and the sunshine came back and Billy fell out retching and gasping for all the air he could reach and hold. Nobody had been cheering.

CHOOSE, BOY. ME OR HIM. DO IT NOW, BOY—I AIN'T GOT ALL DAY.

And that he had chosen the "Me" he only knew later, with Maybelle's help and a Bible College and years spent doing what the Book said he could and should do, seeing for himself its words bring forth a work on dry land he couldn't have even dreamed about seeing done in all his years of groping around in wrestling pools for a feel of underbelly and a tremor and pitch of hissing snout and thrashing tail.

The fiddle was louder behind him in the sanctuary, notes rising up in a way that made the tune sound syncopated, calliope-like and somehow richly placed. And soon the people would begin to arrive, car engines and doors slamming and voices coming up the walkway from the parking lot, all moving together into a chorus of praise, wrapped in an unspoken language of personal need and urged along by the invisible wings of a power that had reached down to him where he was and saved him from the deep and told him what to do to quit the water for the land.

The Rehearsal

The sanctuary still smelled of popcorn, a few stray kernels peeping out from under the back row of pews as Maybelle Manatee carried her fiddle down to her place off the side aisle. It was early; the rest of the band members were not due to arrive for at least another hour and she needed the extra time. The songs her daughters wanted to play hurt her fingers and her bowing had begun to come harder and harder in the past year or so. She stopped near the piano and looked back over the empty pews, late afternoon sunlight giving them an almost liquid texture, golden and slightly purple as it passed through the tinted panes of glass in the side windows. She put her battered fiddle case down in the thick carpet near the pulpit, its back pushed up against the ornately carved base and its nose pointed directly toward the electric organ and the drums. She pulled a chair over from the nearest amplifier and sat down. Her fingers needed to warm up a bit from the chilly wind outside.

It was a pleasure just to be in the quiet, last night's youth program lasting much longer than she had expected and the music sounding strange and at times so loud that the words of praise to the Lord got lost in the crash of drums and sliding whine of electric guitars. Her husband

and daughters had loved every minute of it, Billy in particular seeming to grow stronger and more joyous the louder the music got and the more the young people clapped and sang. But she sometimes liked to remember how it once had been, back when they had started out, just the two of them then with the half-rusted truck Billy had bought second-hand pulling a trailer so old that it shuddered in the wind and screeched and groaned on hills and curves like it was alive but fixing to die just as soon as it could.

And they would go from town to town, meeting to meeting, helping pastors and evangelists and sometimes staying a week or two if Revival broke out, the trailer serving as bedroom and kitchen and a private place to pray with the people who wanted free from whatever it was that kept them deep in sin—praying then hard and clear until the Holy Ghost moved in, busting through it all to bring them to a perfect time to heal. And all through those years she had played her fiddle in whatever band the host churches had got up for the meeting or sometimes alone when there was no band or sometimes not at all in the places where the fiddle was not allowed, singing then instead and later helping with the healing service and with the women, young and old, who needed extra prayer or words of comfort or just a hug and a smile that said somebody understood and wanted very much to see their lives made whole.

She flexed her fingers and watched the slender wedding band catch the light and tried to remember how she had been in an even earlier time, how she had looked and sounded and felt in the days before there was a Billy Manatee and a mutual love that gave the Word of God a deepening which had never gone away.

The music had been there, from almost the earliest moment she could remember, her father seeming to gather it to himself like some people gather stamps or dead butterflies or souvenir cups and saucers from all the places they had been. She was the last child of seven with three other sisters and three brothers, most of them now dead from war or sickness or accidents on the road. But through it all, through the times of joy and the times when the darkness grew so powerful a thing that it could be touched and tasted, the music had gone on sounding out in the old farmhouse and in the scattered meetings her father had tended, his fiddle and guitar and banjo able to push back whatever sadness or pain he came upon almost from the moment he stood up to play. And he had taught her to do what he did, to finger and bow and make the notes flash like bullets wrapped in fire and smoke and coming out of a rifle skillfully aimed and confidently triggered. He took her with him in his old Ford truck when she got old enough to travel, her mother and the others left to work the farm, and together they traveled the mountain roads, his voice sometimes so loud in song or scripture shouts that the squirrels and birds all scattered and the people in the cabins came out to stand and stare when he went chugging by.

She stood up and stretched and walked the few feet to the pulpit. The fiddle case looked dark against the pale blue of the carpet, like a bloated boat riding too low in the water for easy steerage. Her fingers still felt stiff, slightly swollen from the changing weather, but it was getting closer to the time for the others to arrive. She knelt down and ran her fingers over the side of the case, the latches showing rust spots and the leather feeling rough, cuts and dents forming a kind of pattern, a lopsided spider web that began at the front and fanned out toward the back in ever thinner lines.

But the fiddle still shown bright in its red plush bed and the bow felt just right in her hand as she carried them both back over to the chair and sat down fingering the strings the way her father had done while he waited on the preachers to begin.

In memory, it seemed that his fingers had never quit moving, even in between the songs and sitting as he always did close by the pulpit, a little bit apart from whoever had come there to help him, herself included more and more as her own fingers grew long enough to do some good, on second fiddle then, or on banjo or guitar and in the bigger places on piano or foot-pedal organ and toward the very end on drums and sometimes mandolin. He couldn't keep his body still, tapping and shuffling, fingers and boots, to make a kind of music that never got in the way of prayer or threw the preacher off his rhythm when the meetings heated up and the fire of God came down.

She nestled the fiddle in the crook of her arm and let her bow bring back at least a little bit of how it was, her own notes spiraling up into the golden-looking air of the sanctuary as if in search of others of their kind, to join them there and make an Invitation that the angels liked to sing.

> *Sinners, come unto the Lord,*
> *Sinners, come unto the Lord—*

He often danced before the Lord, bow pumping up above his head and big boots thumping out a rough harmony to the straight notes coming through the fiddle and his hair jiggling down over his forehead and hiding his eyes and all the people whooping like God Himself had just peeped in through a window or come down through the roof to rest a moment on the altar and gather in His sheep all by Himself.

—don't you let this moment pass
and lose your soul at last—

And the air would grow hot, even on the coldest day seeming to bypass the rest of the winter months and bring everything into a feeling like August but hotter even than that and well beyond the power of whatever kerosene or coal or wood fire they used to keep the cold outside.

Crying holy unto the Lord—
Crying holy unto the Lord—

The faces of the people made her want to cry, in matching joy for joy and not from any fear or pain as her smaller fingers tried to keep to the pace her father set and her skinny legs knocked together beneath the long dresses her mother made her wear and her green eyes grew wider and wider the nearer to God the meeting came.

If I could, I surely would—
Stand on the Rock—praise God—where
Moses stood—

He sometimes let the bow fall flat down on the strings to grind and twist there until notes came out that she had never shaped as well no matter how she tried in all the years she traveled with the Gospel bands and played the places he would never go. And toward the end he put the fiddle up, letting it rest on the mantelpiece at home and began instead to read and re-read the Book of Psalms.

Crying holy unto the Lord—
Crying holy unto the Lord—

He had died before the first real tour began—leaving her on a day in early spring with her bags all packed and ready for a circuit of the South and one trip north to Cincinnati—from him, right at the end a sudden gasping sound that came and took away the story and the music left to play.

> *Four and twenty Elders bowing all around*
> *the altar,*
> *crying holy unto the Lord—*

Her mother had taken the fiddle down and given it to her on the afternoon that first band had left for Atlanta. And it had traveled with her ever since, cared for but until Billy appeared not often played, other fiddles taking its place in the many different bands during what now seemed a time not quite real, a time of slick and glittered TV-shows and all-night Gospel sings, of studio work and packaged State Department tours, the former power of its music growing weaker in her mind the less she saw of cabin churches and sawdust floors and people's faces red and glowing from the visitation of the Lord.

But even the remembered power of that Lord had all but gone away when she found Billy, at first only a slick-looking brown blur of a body that came up from the darkness of a pool still holding to the jaws of a giant gator and screaming out for help so loud that even the top row of tourists could plainly hear, and later telling her again and again how God had touched him deep down in the water and told him what he ought to do.

She shifted the fiddle into a proper placement underneath her chin and tried to make her fingers move in the rhythms she had heard last night. But nothing seemed to work, her bow bringing out a sound that jarred the silence in the sanctuary like an aging alarm clock in the darkness of a cold winter's morning. It was easier to move in the older ways and keep her memories free.

Keep on the firing line, oh yes—
Just keep on the firing line—

And she had helped Billy do what he was told to do in the darkness and the water, standing by him through each step it took to reach a place where they could plant a crop and tend the fields and move together toward the solid promise of the harvest-time.

Time is running short, Jesus coming soon,
brother
—keep on the firing-line—

She stood and felt the notes leaving the old fiddle in an encircling flight of sound that seemed to whirl and tumble along over the ceiling and the great wooden sword mounted high up on the back wall and then in lesser eddies of itself in among the chandeliers above the center aisle and all the way back to come down quickly on the altar and the pulpit with her husband's Bible resting there, and in a proper closing of its circuit washing finally over piano, drums, and organ and the places where her daughters and their friends would stand and play.

The Right Kind of Ending

-i-

The dog had circled a small clump of palmettos and then stopped, standing in a half-crouch in the semicircle of shade thrown by the stand of young pines that bordered the parsonage grounds. It seemed to be waiting for some signal, a call or whistle which perhaps only it would know meant to keep going or turn back toward the direction of the marshes. From his study window, the Reverend Lail Pergnum watched the dog slowly raise its head and sniff the air. It was an hour past dawn and already looked hot outside, a Sunday morning in July with the church air-conditioning broken down and most of the congregation on vacation.

"What's out there?"

"What? Oh—nothing. A dog." His wife's voice had startled him. She seldom bothered him in the study on Sunday mornings.

"Breakfast's about ready."

"I'll be along." He turned in time to see the hem of her robe flutter around the door facing. His unfinished sermon lay in sections on the desk, a thick pen half-buried in knots of crumpled paper. For almost three days, the "Parable of the Talents" had refused to come into sync with his own prose. He returned to the window just as the dog flopped down in the sand and began to roll side to side on its back.

Last night had been a restless one, his wife's snores and contented grunts irritating him, at first mildly and then with a force as great as a shovel scraping across sandy concrete. He had finally gotten up and tried to work on the sermon but the night sounds quickly took away his concentration and he instead began reading a collection of short stories. It had been cool in the den, the air-conditioning unit softly humming and pinging in a side window and for a time he had been able to forget about the sermon and the coming service and allow himself to travel with the characters of some unfamiliar writer as they pushed their way through a story that seemed to have no possibility of the right kind of ending. He hadn't bothered to finish it.

Outside, now, in the strengthening sunlight, the dog rested on its belly and resumed its waiting. Mr. Pergnum could smell the bacon and hear his wife humming fragments of popular songs, almost recognizable tunes which shifted pitches the louder they grew. He wondered where the dog lived. It seemed to appear only in the early morning, just behind the dawn and always coming from the marshes or the swamp in what Mr. Pergnum had finally decided was less a run than a stumbling lope. But it had never gone beyond the pines and palmetto, seeming to be pulled short of the manicured parsonage lawn as if by some unseen leash or hidden wire and made to roll in the sand or sit up and stare out at things only it apparently could see. And then, after a time, it would slowly raise itself, legs sometimes wide apart, and shake its head and stumble-lope back through the underbrush toward the swamp or the marshes and perhaps beyond to whatever home was there. It had been like that for days as the dog kept coming back and the sermon kept slipping away, and the nights grew longer and more cluttered with unfinished stories. His wife reappeared at the door behind him, her voice providing a peculiar accompaniment to the dog's attempts to stand up.

"How many pieces of French toast?" And then the dog clambered up and ran and seemed to take with him the last distraction between desk and pulpit. The text was speaking clearly and painfully to Mr. Pergnum as he stared at his wife and tried to bring back her words.

"Did you hear?" She tried to smile but it got caught up in a dry cough.

"What?" He glanced back at the window but the dog had disappeared, leaving in the place where it had been three servants and a stern-looking Master positioning themselves as if for the dress rehearsal of an amateur play. The Master looked much like an unpopular ethics professor at seminary. The text again began to slip away.

"How many pieces of French toast?"

"French toast?" The players were lost in the sunlight, bacon and eggs and rich batter coming to crowd out even the remembered portion of the scene. "I thought we were having pancakes. We always have pancakes." He noticed the thick pen, appearing now to be sinking beneath paper waves on his cluttered desk.

He decided to read the Scripture and call for meditation and get everyone home before the air-conditioning was missed.

-ii-

The dog headed south instead of north this time, at one point crashing through a cluster of stunted live-oaks to mingle bark and fur in the air behind. The scent was stronger the closer he came to Sutter's Trail and even the reverberation of gunshots from somewhere out in the swamp did not slow him down until he crested the short bluffs above the shack and came to a stop in the shade, slowly moving his head upwards and lingering each time the scent came clean. A church bell sounded from beyond the pines on the far side of the shack, steady peals, deep and blurring into each other whenever the warm sea-breeze grew stronger. He settled himself slowly down on a bed of pine needles and cocked his head, watching the old man carefully step off the back porch and approach one of two black kettles, thick smoke curling around its sides before being pulled sharply up and away. The dog licked his lips and waited.

-iii-

The church choir room was damp and smelled of mold and Mr. Pergnum bruised his thumb trying to pry open one of the windows. No one had come to Sunday school and the organist had put on the automatic chimes and taken what there was of the choir to the Seahorse Café for donuts and coffee. Mr. Pergnum poked around in the secretary's desk for the key to the supply room (where he thought some electric fans were stored), but she apparently had put it in the one drawer he couldn't open. He finally gave up and went into his private office and tried to re-read the "Parable of the Talents." The bell tunes sounded like they were being sent up from the bottom of a deep well. It was already hot in the office, and his shirt collar felt like it was steadily cutting its way toward bone. For some reason, he thought of the dog and tried to picture where it had gone, to follow it in his mind right through the dense underbrush and down into the swamp or marshes and perhaps all the way to the place the Master and servants had gone when the sunlight touched their shapes back home before breakfast. But sweat blurred his vision, and he wiped it away and tried to name the tunes that whirred and chimed one after another into the humid air outside.

"Lail?" His wife's voice was louder than the chimes.

"In here."

"It's hot. Why don't you open some windows?" She stopped just inside the door and patted at her cheeks with a blue silk handkerchief. Her hair looked wilted, a few strands stuck severely to the sides of her neck.

"I tried out there. I think they're all painted shut. How is it in the sanctuary?"

"Not as bad as in here. Where's Tommy?" She sat down in a wing-backed chair near the desk.

"Eating donuts by now." He shut his Bible mid-sentence, cutting off the smug answer of the first servant. The heat had become almost frightening, a moist heaviness pressing into him that made him wish he was back home in the study. His wife lit a cigarette and stretched her legs, sandal heels rubbing into the deep-piled carpet. He wondered if the dog had reached its home and was even now cooling its belly in a favorite wallow. The desk lamp threw out a light that somehow emphasized the heat, making bookcases and furniture seem from his angle of vision to be tapestry-like, dry blotches of color over which motes washed in moving and latticed shafts of sunlight.

"Fourth of July. Same as last year." She tapped the end of her cigarette against the edge of a rose-shaped ashtray that had been pushed almost to the edge of a small table near her chair. "When will the air be back on?"

"Next week." In recent months, he had begun to look over at her whenever a pause came in his sermon and the people grew restless. More and more often he had seen something there, a lifeless quality about the eyes or mouth that touched him and seemed to linger on past the service and their midday meal and the long, quiet afternoon to almost spring out at him later when he brushed his teeth and examined his own face in the mirror before bedtime. She seemed to be waiting, like the dog in the backyard, patiently resting and watching to see what might come next. He wished the air-conditioning was working.

-iv-

The dog liked to hide down behind the mound of sun-bleached tires near the kettles and watch as the old man dumped in whatever he had managed to get cheap that week from the fish markets on the pier. He sometimes caught the scent from as far away as the beach past the marshes and sometimes he just seemed to know that next morning would find the kettles smoking and simmering and a shiny tin plate set to one side as if he had been expected. And after a while a thick ladle would be rammed down into the kettle, and they would eat in silence, separated by tires or fishnets or parts of old engines, until it was time to sleep.

The old man noticed him and clucked a few times with his tongue. But the dog stayed behind the tires, resting on his belly with his ears flattened forward. He didn't hear the two men come out of the woods behind him and kneel down on the ridge of the bluffs, rifle butts pushing gently into the soft sand. Three cars and a truck pulled off the Ocean Highway one after another and began to push through the gravel and dust toward the shack. The dog raised his head and inched closer to the tires as the truck pulled even with the front porch and the driver whistled at him. It was the first time people had come to the party.

-v-

Mr. Pergnum sat reading in his study, trying to ignore the occasional sound of fireworks or gunshots that came sporadically from the direction of the town. Having just put away the supper dishes, his wife was sitting on the screened-in side porch watching a small television set flicker out a love story while the crickets and tree frogs chirped and clacked outside. The afternoon had been a long one, the house offensively quiet and no clouds in the sky and darkness hours away.

He closed the book of stories and walked to the air-conditioner. The cool felt good against his neck and face, and he shut his eyes and tried to forget the morning service with its depleted choir and three-person congregation and his wife's eyes as they focused on him during the benediction. He felt that his words had echoed about in the beauty of the sanctuary like birds let inside a house by mistake, and he had wanted to call each one of them back before they could come to roost. He had been ten years in this Presbytery, a time of golf and fishing and slow-paced comfort, the exact contours of which had only that morning raised themselves sufficiently to let him see as well as feel how far along he was, how much past the point in his own story where surprises of fresh beginnings could be expected, where stray dogs and strained visions could be made more than chance interruptions in the rhythm of a low Sunday morning. His wife's eyes had told him all that and made him want more than ever to run with the dog and follow its lead until they perhaps caught the strengthening scent of the elusive and confusing Master and his servants, and then to track together for a time before falling down into a dreamless sleep somewhere short of a final destination.

"Let's go watch the sunset." His wife's voice sounded tired. He hadn't heard her come inside.

"Is it pretty?"

"Trying to be. It's even hot in here. We can sit on the stoop and listen to the fireworks. Maybe some air will stir."

"Get the mosquito repellant." He tried but couldn't see her eyes as she stretched her arms over her head and smiled.

-vi-

The dog lay sleeping just beyond the circle of light thrown by the bonfire. Mosquito whines sounded like tiny ambulance sirens amid the night noise from the nearby swamp and the loud talk of the people gathered around the kettles. He had eaten everything they gave him and even let the old man pat him once on the head as the last portion was ladled hot onto a flattened pie plate. The people were singing now or laughing between long sips of beer, and a breeze had come in fresh and cool from a storm far out to sea. Further down the highway the town fireworks had begun and deep thumps and whining shrieks mingled for a time with all the other noises until the people got quiet and tried to guess when the next one would come. The dog sucked at the scraps of his chowder and glanced over at the old man, a tall silhouette near a ruined boat, and hoped the people would stay until morning.

ACKNOWLEDGMENTS

Having long ago granted the unwavering and primary guidance of Jesus Christ, my own Lord, Savior, and ultimate Creator, I would also like to thank the following people, living and dead, who in various ways figure into the making of these specific stories:

-----First and enduring thanks go to my maternal grandfather, Mr. Hiram Benjamin Conner, proud Georgian, southern gentleman, master story-teller, and a man who established a love in his first grandson for both history and the South.

-----Alexander Pope, master of satire, who broke the back of the patronage system in eighteenth-century England.

-----Pastors Richard and Darlene Little for taking me into their home when I was homeless. "The Gator and the Holy Ghost" the story and "The Rehearsal" are dedicated to them. I would also like to thank the members of Faith Christian Assembly/Wilkesboro, NC (at least the membership back in the mid-to late 1980s—especially Reverend Steve Prevette) who kept me going through such *kindnesses as the purchase of a typewriter (when mine had died) and through various opportunities for productive labor. Along these lines, I would also like to thank Fathers Putnam and Walsh in the Diocese of Charlotte for services only they would know—and for helping me continue writing at a time when all seemed lost (something they most likely are not aware of).*

-----*Since the stories in this first collection were written mostly between 1970—2011, the following people figure prominently, in one way or another (and in no real order of importance) in its creation: Aubrey Williams (one of the authentic greats), Smith Kirkpatrick (for teaching me the importance of titles), Ward Hellstrom, Howard Greenfeld (whose letters of encouragement shone brightly indeed), Rosalie Siegel, Guy Blynn (whose friendship and encouragement mean more than he knows and whose advice to put my fiction online was finally heeded), John Swanger and Linda Taylor and Barbara Kolarik (who listened back in a time when very few did), Bob Collins and Mike Romig—good friends and former Kirby Knob Boys, Lonnie Bumgarner (the true renaissance man and a superb critic), Ann Compton Fortuna, Pam D. Shumate, Dorothy Grimes (who provided shelter for my family and me and who taught me the proper way to paint a house), Randy Candelaria (consummate professional and superb teacher of the techniques of research), Tom Gordon (lover of books and a fellow Kingston Trio zealot), Kathleen Malone, Lydia Kirkland (talented writer and graduate of the Lake Lucina school of storytelling), Chuck Snoak, Susie Keener (one of the very best: honest and courageously Christian), Anthony Russell (whose many timely kindnesses can never be perfectly repaid), Steven Weav-*

er, Lin Fain, Kristin Redfield, Shari Covitz, Drew Rowe, Linda Lee, Allen Pinnix (a friend who has become family and in whose debt I will always remain), Sylvia Haith (fellow soldier in the fight for meaningful equality), Phllip Carter (steadfast advocate for justice), Elaine Hage (a dear friend who suffers my eccentricity), R. Wayne Fortuna (in deep thanks for his example and service as an honest teacher of history in a most difficult environment, and for remaining my favorite brother in spite of the assaults of time and distance), Carolyn Fortuna (many, many thanks for the cover design of this collection—a cover she created from rather vague suggestions and a piece of work that only gives a brief view of her talent), my children (Catherine Compton, Richard, and Mike Shay), Denise White (for courage and leadership in the ongoing fight), Debbie Pritchard (stalwart comrade-in-arms and superb teacher), Greg Chase (who never shirks his duty), Yolanda Wilson (who brings order out of chaos and leads by example), special thanks to Bill and Mona Cofer and to Gwen Whitaker, Cheri Silverman (who has saved many a day without being properly thanked), Amy Quesenberry (a steadfast friend, honest and true), and all my colleagues and friends who, if not mentioned here, know who they are and know my thanks. And please note that if I go to a future volume of stories and send out the novels as well, there will be ample space and time to thank many more than are mentioned here.

-----*Before ending this thank-a-thon, however, I would like to mention in a special way my editor and friend, Chris Brincefield. Without Chris's encouragement and most especially without his keen criticism story by story, minutely at times, and more general when necessary, this*

*collection would not have come together—but rather
would have continued to collect dust waiting to be either
carted out to the street or burned with kindling on a cold,
winter's night (and some might say that would at least
have been a useful ending!). Thanks, Chris, for not giving
up on an old man with far too many manuscripts and far
too little time left to maneuver them through the treach-
erous waters of traditional publication. Let the public directly decide!*

-----*And, finally, my wife, Kathleen, shines the brightest of all the
rest, a woman of keen intellect and deep compassion
who somehow saw something worth salvaging in a rather tattered teacher/writer and has given him a reason
to continue to write, but more importantly, a reason to
live. And to her the Collection is dedicated.*

*James L. Fortuna, Jr.
June 11, 2012
Winston-Salem, NC*

About James L. Fortuna, Jr.

Born: Jacksonville, Florida. Oct. 6, 1943---product of WWII—
Italian New-Englander father and a Scots-Irish south
Georgia mother. A mix of Garibaldi and the Confederacy.

Raised briefly in Maine (1946-1950)---longer time in North Florida—Jacksonville/ with some in north central Florida,
Gainesville (college). Span: 1950—1977. 1977 to present
in western North Carolina.

Began as an ardent white supremacist/ segregationist/and a
states-rights advocate—now: a recovering racist—and,
as of April 30, 2005: an honorary African-American. An
interesting journey all in all.

Education: Mostly in Florida. 4 degrees from Univ. of Fla—
including a Ph.D in eighteenth-century English literature.
Book published on Samuel Richardson's "Pamela."
Taught: (1). Univ. of Fla. (2). Wilkes Community College
(3). Forsyth Technical Community College. (4). Adjunct at
Salem College—Winston-Salem, NC.

Work: Congressional page (Eisenhower's last congress)/ House
painter—exterior and interior/ shovel hand—
Smithsonian—South Dakota/ Print shop worker/ parking
lot attendant/ mail room worker/light meter read-

er/manual labor jobs—misc.—yard work and gardening/ carpenter's assistant/ garbage remover/ primary care of my infant daughter 1975-1981 (manual laboring jobs and part-time teaching during this period in particular).

Teaching assignments: English (all kinds)—history—sociology— psychology—religion—philosophy—the Holocaust— ethics.

Other facts: lived for a brief while in a new age commune----- have taught Sunday school to pre-schoolers and adults both-----worked as a state officer in LBJ bid for presidency in 1960-----worked as a state officer in JFK/LBJ campaign in 1960. 1963—to the present: an advocate for civil rights—became homeless in 1985 after a series of bad personal decisions and a civil rights lawsuit against a college. During that time period continued to write (bulk of my novels came then), continued with manual laboring jobs and part-time teaching—until hired full-time by Forsyth Tech in 1994; am still there.-----Homeless advocate—1984—present (off and on)-----play at the 5-string banjo (old-timey style)-----gardening (vegetables and flowers)—especially like family, friends, and animals----- a seasoned warrior in the fight for fairness and justice----- -enjoy lively intellectual discussion—as noted above: have written ten novels and countless short stories (mostly on the fly and homeless and in between teaching assignments)—am pretty much a straightforward Christian---and: I love my wife.

Don't miss the next story collection

by

James L. Fortuna Jr.

A Burning of Ducks and Other Stories

…coming soon from

Lightnin' Bug Publishing